This poor man. Gaia almost smiled again. He was still living under the delusion that he had control over his life—control over Gaia, control over this other woman. He still believed that he could force his will upon the world. Another hopeless sap, a sagging mountain of testosterone gone awry. Was the old cliché really true, that men were really all the same? Certainly the men in her life didn't rate much higher than Pudgy Jogging Suit here. Sure, they weren't brutal rapists. But they had other faults going for them. Unreliability. Dishonesty. Cruelty.

Kicking this guy's ass would be a pleasure. A way to take revenge upon all the slimeballs who made the world a more foul place, her father included. Yes, maybe this was her purpose in life: to teach the men of the world a lesson—that they were all swine, each in their own unique fashion.

Gaia's eyes flashed to the guy's victim. She was frozen, eyes wide, uncomprehending.

He took a step forward. "Come and get some, sweetheart," he whispered.

Don't miss any books in this thrilling new series
from Pocket Books:

FEARLESS™

#1 Fearless
#2 Sam
#3 Run
#4 Twisted
#5 Kiss
#6 Payback
#7 Rebel
#8 Heat
#9 Blood
#10 Liar
#11 Trust
#12 Killer
#13 Bad
#14 Missing
#15 Tears
#16 Naked

All Pocket Book titles are available by post from:
**Simon & Schuster Cash Sales, P.O. Box 29,
Douglas, Isle of Man IM99 1BQ**
Credit cards accepted. Please telephone 01624 836000,
Fax 01624 670923, Internet http://www.bookpost.co.uk
or email: bookshop@enterprise.net for details

FEARLESS™

FRANCINE PASCAL

NAKED

POCKET
BOOKS

To Michael & Ada Rubin

An imprint of Simon & Schuster UK Ltd
A Viacom Company
Africa House, 64-78 Kingsway, London WC2B 6AH

Produced by 17th Street Productions, Inc.
33 West 17th Street, New York, NY 10011

A CIP catalogue record for this book is
available from the British Library

ISBN 07434 15388

1 3 5 7 9 10 8 6 4 2

Printed and bound in Great Britain by Omnia Books Ltd, Glasgow

A funny thing happened to me the other day. (Was it yesterday?) I woke up, showered, scarfed down two bowls of Froot Loops, and went to school. For some reason, though, the doors were locked and the building was empty.

And then I remembered. It was Saturday.

Ha ha ha. Hysterical, right?

Guess you had to be there.

I can't seem to keep track of time anymore. For example, I know my father left a few days ago. I'm just not sure how many days it was. Four? Five? Six? Not that it matters. He'll probably be gone for another five years, or ten, or forever. And I suspect that if I had some adult supervision—if I weren't just living in solitude in a big, two-bedroom sublet on Mercer Street—I probably would have a better idea of where I should be, or where I'd been, and when.

But I don't. Have any adult supervision, that is.

Yes, that's right. For the first time in my life, I am completely responsible for myself. What freedom. I am free to stuff my face full of doughnuts at any time. I am free to watch mindless TV for hours on end. I am free to cry whenever I want. In fact, crying is the activity that seems to take up most of my time. It's a little odd, seeing as I can probably count on one hand the number of times I cried in the last five years. Unfortunately, it also makes me feel like a loser: pathetic, lame, and weak. And ironically, when I experience these emotions, I just want to cry some more.

So that's precisely what I do.

No wonder I've always fantasized about living on my own. It's nonstop fun!

George Niven wants me to move back in with him, back into the brownstone on Perry Street. He checks up on me every single night. Of course, I'd rather

spend an eternity in hell than
move back into that house, but I
keep that to myself. I just make
up excuses about how I'm too busy
to pack, et cetera. (That's
another disturbing trend I've
noticed: I've started to tell
little lies all the time.) I feel
too sorry for him to tell him the
truth. I empathize with him. I
know what he's going through.
He's all alone.

It's all very humorous on some
level. I mean, I can be calm in a
hostage situation. Put me up against
some knife-wielding skinheads, and
I'll be cool as a proverbial cucum-
ber. But day to day. . . trying to
fall asleep in this apartment,
trying to walk to Gray's Papaya,
trying to make it through a single
class at school. . . I never know
what I'm going to get. Tears?
Rage? The sudden and desperate
need to leave the room?
Anything's possible.

And if I could feel fear, I
would be afraid—mostly of myself.

Because I've entered unchartered territory. I used to be completely in control. Well, not always, but I was usually in control enough to maintain a smooth, icy veneer as far as the outside world was concerned. But now I'm living this precarious existence where I'm one step away from losing my shit at all times.

What I wouldn't give for the days when I used to feel nothing—back when I had all my emotions folded up and packed away in a nice big steel trunk in my head. Back when I could go through *months* without crying. Hell, there were probably two years there where I didn't feel much of anything at all. Those were the days.

But now, thanks to the many men in my life (my father, Sam, my uncle Oliver, Ed), I have no control over my feelings anymore. These men tricked me. That's what it basically comes down to. They snuck up on me, tempted me with happiness (as if such a thing actually exists), and then collectively broke my heart. They abandoned me. Not just once, either. My father abandoned me *twice*. It's as if they all took a secret meeting at some big hunting lodge—you know, the ones with the red walls and those huge antlers and disgusting mounted deer heads—and conspired to screw with my head: to pick the lock on my steel trunk, to drag out every single emotion I've ever had and hang it on display for the general public.

But enough about them.

Have you ever tried a doughnut shake? Neither had I until the other day. (Or was that earlier today?) Anyway, I was standing at my disgusting kitchen counter with a box of one dozen assorted Krispy Kreme doughnuts in one hand and a half gallon of milk in the other. Lunch. (Or was it dinner?) And then I saw the blender.

Three seconds later I was

stuffing doughnuts down into the large Pyrex blender cup—cinnamon, jelly, chocolate glazed, Boston cream, powdered—as many as I could. Then I poured in as much milk as I could, secured the rubber lid, and slammed down every button on that blender—mix, chop, puree, *congeal*, whatever. . . . I watched as all those doughnuts turned into a thick and lumpy vomit-colored sludge, and then I hurled off the lid, lifted the entire concoction to my mouth, and took a "sip."

Needless to say, it was the most horrifying dose of concentrated sugar I'd ever tasted. But as I spat the sludge out into the sink full of dishes. . . I realized. . .

That doughnut shake was a perfect metaphor for what is clearly the true chaos of human existence. I'm sure you see what I mean.

It's like that book we've been reading in MacGregor's English

class. Camus's *The Stranger*.
Everything Camus wrote is dead-
on. There's no *order* to anything.
There's no *reason* for anything.
It's all just one long list of
absurd events with no payoff
whatsoever. Feel what you want;
it doesn't matter. Do what you
want; it doesn't matter.

I can't believe how much time
I've wasted thinking my life was
leading somewhere in particular,
thinking there was some kind of
master plan for me—as if there
was ever a "right" or a "wrong"
thing for me to do. There's no
meaning to any of it. We're all
just a bunch of random doughnuts,
crammed into this giant blender
for no apparent reason, chopped
at, spun around, and blended
together into a repulsive and
utterly meaningless *mud*.

So from now on, as far as I'm
concerned, the more absurd, the
better. I'll just do and feel
nothing and everything at the
same time, in giant swirls and

spins and stops and starts. No
control over a stitch of it. I'll
cry and then I'll be numb, and
then I'll feel so unbelievably
pissed off, I'll want to rip my
door off its hinges and break
every breakable item in this
empty apartment. One hundred percent pure emotional free fall—
total chaos in my brain. Thank
you all so very much.

Control. Isn't it ridiculous?
People are always trying to take
control of themselves or else
they're trying to control someone
else. They're all so deluded.
When are they going to learn?
There's simply no such thing as
control. None at all.

Sure, they weren't brutal rapists. But they had other faults **human** going **garbage** for them. Unreliability. Dishonesty. Cruelty.

THE SUN WAS THREATENING TO show itself.

Gaia kept praying the night would last just a little longer. Somehow the days were worse than the nights. People usually complained that the opposite was true; after all, there must have been a

Scum Exodus

thousand sad, lame, cheesy songs about "lonely nights." But Gaia found the sunny days so much more depressing. All those kids screaming and laughing in the playgrounds. What the hell made them so happy that they had to scream? Was it the melting black sludge that lined the sidewalks—the last remnants of snow? Or the litter? The torn coffee cups and discarded syringes? The filth that seemed to ooze from every stinking corner of this city?

That was the problem with the days: You could see every miserable detail so clearly. Yet somehow the real garbage—the *human* garbage—managed to stay indoors.

Night was different, though. At night the scum of New York scurried out of their little holes and crevices and wrought havoc. Just like cockroaches. Turn out the lights, and they all came out to party. Turn the lights back on, and they all vanished. Judging from the deep blue of the predawn sky, Gaia had only another half hour or so before the sun came out and the scum exodus began. She still hadn't cracked any heads.

As long as there were psychos and sickos to pummel, Gaia had a hobby to occupy the meaningless and seemingly endless hours of solitude. Sleep had become a nonissue. Sleep was for the weak. Actually, she had simply been incapable of sleeping for the last few nights (four, five, six?). Which was why she was roaming Avenue D and Ninth Street at five-thirty in the morning again. Looking to kick the asses of the bad guys.

Alphabet City seemed to be mapped out specifically for crime. The farther down the alphabet you went, the more crime you found. Avenue B was worse than Avenue A, Avenue C was worse than Avenue B, and so on. And after midnight. . . forget about it. You might as well wear a sign saying, "Sell me drugs or mug me, please." Perfect for Gaia. *Question: What do you call a young blond girl, alone on Avenue D after midnight? Answer: Bait.*

There had already been one attempt to mug her. One very lame attempt. A guy had pushed her into a dark alley, hoping to do God knows what. Gaia hadn't even had to engage the poor idiot in combat, though; after she'd disarmed him—kicking the knife from his hands with a left jump kick—he'd taken off into the shadows. But there was usually more action—

"Get back in the car, bitch!"

11

Gaia swung her head around.

Not twenty feet behind her, a pudgy, balding guy in one of those neo-mafia-style jogging suits had forced a woman in a tight red dress against the hood of a beat-up car. A flicker of adrenaline leaped through Gaia's body. *Finally,* she thought, unable to keep from smiling. It was about time.

"I don't think the date's over until I say it's over," the guy hissed.

"Stop it," the woman cried, desperately struggling to wriggle away from him. "You're drunk!"

Gaia could hear the plaintive note of fear in the woman's voice, wondering even as she broke into a sprint what it must be like to feel *afraid*. . . afraid of this ridiculously overbuffed oaf. Energy surged through her veins as she rocketed toward them. Now the guy was forcing himself on the woman, leaning into her and slobbering all over her with sloppy kisses.

"Stop it!" she shrieked, squirming. "Stop—"

"Shut up and stay still! You're just making it worse."

No, you are, Gaia retorted silently. She threw the full weight of her body against him, grabbing his shoulder with one hand, spinning, tearing him away from his victim.

"What the hell?" he shouted, eyes blazing.

His gaze locked with Gaia's. For a moment he just gaped at her, breathing hard. Then he smiled.

"Cool," he muttered. "A threesome."

This poor man. Gaia almost smiled again. He was still living under the delusion that he had control over his life—control over Gaia, control over this other woman. He still believed that he could force his will upon the world. Another hopeless sap, a sagging mountain of testosterone gone awry. Was the old cliché really true, that men were really all the same? Certainly the men in her life didn't rate much higher than Pudgy Jogging Suit here. Sure, they weren't brutal rapists. But they had other faults going for them. Unreliability. Dishonesty. Cruelty.

Kicking this guy's ass would be a pleasure. A way to take revenge upon all the slimeballs who made the world a more foul place, her father included. Yes, maybe this was her purpose in life: to teach the men of the world a lesson—that they were all swine, each in their own unique fashion.

Gaia's eyes flashed to the guy's victim. She was frozen, eyes wide, uncomprehending.

He took a step forward. "Come and get some, sweetheart," he whispered.

"Don't mind if I do," Gaia said. She grabbed his wrist, yanking him off balance. His eyes widened. Before he could react, she'd used the momentum of his fall against him, whirling and flipping him on his backside. All two hundred and fifty pounds of flesh slammed to the pavement, hitting with a smack.

"Shit!" he howled. "What the—"

A swift kick to the ribs silenced him. He writhed helplessly on the sidewalk, looking less like a human and more like some kind of animal, a giant seal, maybe. She kicked him again.

"Help!" he gasped.

Normally Gaia took the minimalist approach to a battle, just as her father had trained her. It was a lesson from the *Go Rin No Sho:* Strike only where and when necessary. Defend yourself, but do no more. Put an end to the struggle—and your opponent will think twice before he attacks again. But tonight there was another feeling creeping up on her, an added and unexpected impulse. . . one that commanded her to increase the pain, even though the competition was a joke. She had just a little less control. . . .

She stared down at him in a fighting stance. She barely noticed the woman in the red dress running away down the street. The second kick definitely wasn't called for. He was terrified now, struggling to crawl away from her on all fours. Why had she given him more than necessary? He was a total nonthreat. Kid stuff. Maybe it was her new philosophy? That nothing mattered at all—that there was no sense to any of it, no point to any of it, so why not give them everything you've got? No mercy.

Maybe . . .

But the feeling ran deeper than that.

Gaia's legs began to go wobbly. It was expected, yet another phenomenon she did not understand—utter exhaustion after a battle. Given the brief and effortless nature of this particular fight, however, Gaia was confident she could make it home without actually fainting. Yes. Already she could feel strength returning. She blinked a few times, then turned and strode down the street, back in the direction of her apartment. The sun finally began to creep up from behind the projects lining the East River—marking the official end to another sleepless night of wandering and makeshift justice.

Not surprisingly, she didn't feel any better.

Best-Laid Plans

LOKI HAD YET TO TAKE CREATURE comforts for granted. He'd only been out of prison for a week, so he could still appreciate a good croissant, a steaming cup of latte. As had become his new morning ritual, he sat alone at the glass table in the dining room of the spacious Chelsea penthouse, picking at his breakfast and staring at the magnificent view of the Hudson River.

And as usual, he whispered a simple mantra.

"Tom is dead."

True, his brother's demise wasn't a reality—not yet. But picturing the body, saying the words. . . somehow these little rites brought the reality a little closer. Loki had suffered long enough. He'd borne more than a man should ever have to bear: a brother who'd stolen his one true love, who'd fathered the daughter that should have rightly been his—who had delayed the greatest work of Loki's career with that unfortunate incarceration.

But that was behind him now. It was time to move forward.

Sighing, he tightened the sash on his bathrobe and booted up the sleek laptop beside his breakfast china. He was anxious to see the morning's status reports from his various contacts, anxious to see the plans that were once more falling into place. But thoughts of his brother lingered.

Once you are dead, Tom, Gaia will be free. Free at last to know who she truly is and all she is meant for.

A wistful smile grew on his face as the computer whirred and hummed, springing to life. The original plan was to kidnap Gaia. He should have known better than that all along. Yet Loki was sure his brother must have brainwashed the girl—filling her head with all kinds of lies about "Uncle Oliver" and what an evil man he was. So naturally, he'd assumed he would have to capture Gaia—to deprogram her, in a way. But it looked like Tom had taken care of that for him.

His smile broadened. Once again his brother's naive, shortsighted devotion to duty had cost him his family. And created the perfect opportunity for Loki to step in. It would only be a matter of time before Gaia would come back to him of her own volition. She needed her flesh and blood. Loki knew that. He couldn't believe how consistently foolish Tom had proven himself to be. Didn't Tom realize that every abandonment only pushed Gaia closer to his brother? Was he really that stupid?

Yes. Of course. Because—

Loki's eyes flashed to the screen. His smile disappeared.

To: L
From: QR4

Enigma has shed surveillance. Backup unsuccessful. Please advise.

Reflexively Loki pounded his fist on the delicate glass table. The china rattled. How could Tom possibly have escaped surveillance? There were four men on him. Four men. Monitoring one fool. Enigma indeed. Any idiot ought to be able to overcome Tom's tragically outdated cloaking tactics. This was an unacceptable glitch. Loki couldn't keep Tom out of the way if he couldn't find him.

He slammed the reply icon and tapped out his response, speaking every word through clenched teeth as he typed.

To: QR4
From: L

    Completely unacceptable. There will be con-
sequences. Check *all* contacts for a possible
leak. If Enigma is out-of-pocket, then he is
searching for information. If leak is discov-
ered, do nothing. Report to me for further
instructions.
    Contact J for briefing. I want a full report
from J confirming that the messenger is still
in hand.
    Do not fail again. You are expendable.

Loki minimized the memo program and quickly clicked open a secure instant message board. If Tom had shed his surveillance, he might very well be planning something for Gaia. Some further impediment to Loki's operation. And that particular notion only served to double Loki's deep frustration. If only he could just dispose of Tom right now. Just remove him from the equation altogether, once and for all.

But at this moment the essential concern was Gaia. Only Gaia.

Instant Message Board 19
QR6-8 Status: Secure 05:25

L: QR6—Report location

QR6: Location—Ninth Street, Avenue D

L: Report on subject

QR6: Subject is repeating pattern for fifth
consecutive night.

Loki's smile returned. Yes, he had no doubt that she would return to him soon, and of her own free will.

Standing Still

"BEEP BEEP, MAN! COMING THROUGH, coming through! Keep *moving*, man!"

Ed Fargo somehow managed to lean out of the way just before the bike messenger lopped off his arm. But in the process of leaning, he lost one crutch—and then, in the process of grabbing for that crutch, he lost the other crutch. And then he fell on his ass in the middle of the sidewalk. *America's Funniest Recovering Paraplegics.*

Only Ed wasn't smiling.

Bike messengers. The scourge of New York City. There seemed to be no greater thrill for a bike messenger than to terrorize pedestrians while speeding down sidewalks at forty miles an hour. Ed watched the guy vanish in a sea of legs, fighting to grab his wayward crutch. Nobody bent to help him. Not that he was particularly surprised. After all, these people were New Yorkers. They had places to be. It was Monday morning in Greenwich Village. There was no time for the meek and injured.

At these times—meaning the times he had to force himself to his feet in a humiliating frenzy of red-faced pain and grunting—he had to remind himself that he was truly lucky. Screw that: he was probably one of the luckiest guys in the world. The experimental surgery had worked. He'd regained use of his legs. True, the word *use* was a little generous at the moment. But the doctors were confident that he'd be able to walk without crutches in a matter of months.

So why do I feel like shit ninety-nine percent of the time?

Actually, he knew the answer to that question. He'd known it the moment he'd jumped from his wheelchair to save Gaia Moore's life over a week ago. Because if the shock of that near-death experience had taught him anything (besides the fact that standing within a ten-foot radius of Gaia Moore was extraordinarily hazardous to one's health), it was that he'd made a trade-off. A very confusing one.

For years Ed had dreamed of once again being just another invisible citizen on the streets of New York. No more gawking at the poor wheelchair boy. But as he lurched back down the street, he wasn't so sure how he felt about his dreams coming true. That be-careful-what-you-wish-for thing kept floating around in his head.

Here you go, he told himself. *You wanted invisible. . . you've got invisible.*

He'd been in the chair so long that he'd actually forgotten how far most New Yorkers took the notion of every man for himself. It could be a lonely feeling. Ed had been dragging himself out for "walks" on these crutches every damn day, hoping to bask in the glory of finally being out of the chair. But every time he was outside, he got the same nagging uneasy feeling: he didn't exist. People had always moved out of his way. Either on his board or in his chair, people had made way for him—just like people had made way for the bike messenger who had almost mowed him down. Now Ed was the one who had to get out of the way. He just couldn't remember any other time in his life when he'd felt so. . . insignificant. Nobody noticed him anymore.

But that wasn't even the worst of the trade-off.

No, the worst of it was that there was one person in this city who would notice Ed more than ever before. One whom he'd managed to avoid for the past week (his parents had allowed him to stay home from school, what with the trauma of the attack in the park). One who would never forgive him. . . .

Heather.

He winced. The Village School loomed down the block. In a matter of minutes he would confront Heather face-to-face. He felt sick. He'd broken his promise. He'd revealed to the world the truth about his surgery. It didn't matter that he'd been justified— that if he hadn't jumped from his wheelchair, both he and Gaia would be dead. No, as far as Heather was concerned, in that one moment he'd screwed the Gannis family out of $26 million. And even though Ed had forced Gaia to keep his secret, he'd neglected to consider just how many kids at the Village School hung out in Washington Square Park. Apparently two had seen the attack. They had seen Ed Fargo on his own two feet. News traveled fast in the West Village. The principal had already called to offer his congratulations, to wish Ed a speedy recovery.

Heather knows.

Ed shook his head, staring down at the gray concrete. Of course she knew. She hadn't called in a week, hadn't dropped by to visit, hadn't e-mailed. She was

22

his girlfriend, and they hadn't communicated once since the incident. Not once—

"Jesus, come on, guy!" a harsh voice spat in Ed's ear. "Keep moving!"

Ed smiled grimly. *Keep moving,* he thought. *Yeah, right.* At this particular moment Ed wasn't really sure he wanted to keep moving. He'd rather just stand still. For a long, long time.

GEORGE, GAIA THOUGHT ANGRILY,  staring at the phone on the kitchen counter, sitting there amidst the discarded hot-dog wrappers and doughnut boxes. Of course it was George. Who else would call so early in the morning? She knew she shouldn't be angry, but she couldn't help it. The guy clearly thought she was a basket case.

And she was, of course. But that was her own goddamn business.

The irritating ring echoed off the bare kitchen walls—ring number four. George was probably checking up to make sure she was going to school. Well, fine. She would reassure him. Yes, she was going to school. And with any luck she would pick a fight, kick some ass, and get expelled. She marched across the sticky kitchen floor and snatched up the phone.

"Hello?" she spat.

"Gaia?"

Not George. A woman's voice. One she didn't recognize.

"Who is this?" Gaia demanded.

"I'm sorry. . . is this Gaia Moore's residence?"

Sorry. What is she sorry about? Who is this woman? Does she know something about my father? Has something happened to him?

"Who is this?" Gaia asked again.

"It's Patricia Moss. Mary Moss's mother."

Time seemed to freeze. A series of images tore through Gaia's head, as rapidly and painfully piercing as machine-gun fire: images of Mary—sitting on her bed, running down the street, laughing with that devilish spark in her eye, tossing her red hair over her shoulder. . . lying dead in a pool of blood.

Mary, her one true friend.

"Gaia?"

"Yes?" Gaia croaked. Her voice was shaking, unrecognizable to herself.

"It is you," Mrs. Moss breathed. "I got this number from George Niven, but the way you answered the phone, I thought. . . well, I thought had the wrong number."

"No, it's me," Gaia whispered.

"Well, good. Mr. Niven told me that you're living with your father now. How's that going?"

Gaia squeezed her eyes shut. *Oh, it's going great. Peachy. Perfect.*

"Gaia?" Mrs. Moss asked.

"Fine," Gaia said, swallowing. A lone tear fell from her cheek.

There was an odd beat of silence on the line. "Are you sure? Mr. Niven mentioned that your father was out of town on business."

"Yeah, well. . . um, he isn't around much, I guess," Gaia stammered.

"Is he there now?"

Gaia sniffed, desperately fighting to maintain control. "No," she whispered, clenching her teeth.

"When is he—"

"I'm living alone," she interrupted, not knowing exactly why she was confessing. She hated unloading her problems on *anyone*, particularly this poor woman. "I mean, I'm living in his apartment, but he's gone. I don't know where."

"Don't you have anyone?" Mrs. Moss pressed.

Gaia drew in a deep, trembling breath. *I thought I had Sam, but he's gone, too.* She shook her head. "Well, not really. I mean, no. I just. . . I'm sorry, Mrs. Moss, I'm sort of out of it." Everything poured from her mouth in a jumble; it was as if her mind was a prison wall that had been blown to smithereens, and her words were escaping prisoners, clambering for freedom. "I'm sure he'll be —"

"Gaia?" Mrs. Moss interrupted gently.

Gaia squeezed her eyes shut. "Yes?"

"Why don't you come and stay with us?"

She blinked, not quite sure if she had heard the question correctly. "Excuse me?"

"Well, I was calling to see if you wanted to come to dinner, but why don't you just stay with us for a while? You know, until your father gets back?"

"You want . . ." Gaia left the sentence hanging. A very strange feeling was welling up deep inside her—a dizzy, vertiginous sensation. . . one that was not entirely unpleasant. But there was no way she could take Mrs. Moss up on her offer. There was no way she would allow herself to impose on another household like that. She would take care of herself. She'd *vowed* to take care of herself.

"We could use the company," Mrs. Moss said, very simply. Her voice seemed to catch. "You know Brendan's at school, but he visits as much as he can. And Paul moved back home from the dorms to be closer to the family. I'm worried about him. He puts on a brave face every day, but when I walk past his room late at night, I can hear him crying. I know he's hurting. We're all spending as much time together as we can, but the apartment still feels so empty, Gaia."

Gaia couldn't speak. The lump in her throat was

too large. She could only nod, glancing around at her own apartment. She knew all about feelings of emptiness.

"Please, Gaia," Mrs. Moss pleaded in the silence. "Please come stay with us. Just for a while. You'd bring such a light to our house, and it would mean so much to me right now. Let us take care of you while your father's out of town."

It was so completely out of left field—so utterly random: a chance for Gaia to be somewhere that had nothing to do with her life. Just pack a bag and escape. It was time to do something new. It was time to be someplace else—a place where she could make others happy. So Gaia didn't even allow herself time to think. She merely acted.

"Okay," she heard herself say, and she immediately felt much better.

My father used to force me to take walks. This was from the age of about seven to ten, before my parents had split up. He'd pull me out of bed at six in the morning, tug a shirt over my head, and drag me outside, telling me some lame fiction about how we were going to search for "little details" along the way, things we hadn't noticed before. In fact, he was just a stickler for regimented exercise.

I hated those walks. I couldn't stand walking if there wasn't a clear destination. What was our goal, our mission? Where were we headed?

But in the last few months long, aimless walks have become my only solace. I suppose it makes sense. With everything I've been through recently, my childhood seems to have fallen much farther away. My whole life has fallen away, really. Well, more like it was ripped away—by Ella Niven, by Josh Kendall, and *whoever*.

SAM

I used to think I had problems: my parents got divorced; I was diagnosed with diabetes. But I had no idea what I was talking about. I no longer consider those problems. In fact, I practically view them as blessings at this point—the trials and challenges of a *normal* life. Those were the kinds of problems I had before I met Gaia Moore.

My life history should really be split into two portions: BG and AG—before Gaia and after Gaia. And year one AG has been a disaster the likes of which I've never experienced. It's just been one long runaway train ride.

That's what it feels like. Like before Gaia, I could at least understand the twists and turns in the track. I knew where the brakes were, and I knew how to navigate. But then, with absolutely no warning, Gaia pops into my life, and then Ella Niven pulls that big steel peg between the cars and cuts me loose from the rest of the train.

Gaia's psycho stepmother started all of this. She got me drunk that one goddamn night, we ended up in bed together, and then she killed one of my best friends. If she hadn't killed Mike, I never would have been a suspect, and I never would have needed an alibi. And if I hadn't needed an alibi, I never would have ended up taking a fake alibi from Josh in exchange for all these nefarious little errands he's been pushing on me. And so it goes, on and on, one little tragedy after the next, rolling by me as I look on, totally powerless.

Now I'm careening down the track, with no brakes, no controls, and no idea where the train is going. When I look behind me, I see the rest of the train shrinking rapidly into the distance. When I look ahead, everything is racing by in such a blur, I can't make out any details.

I wish I had some idea where the hell I was going. I wish I knew how this was all going to end.

She wanted to make him squirm. She wanted to make him feel **utter** like shit. **coldness** Basically, she wanted to hurt him the way he'd hurt her.

SHE HAS TO COME, SAM PRAYED silently. *She can't live without her morning coffee.*

Two Repelling Magnets

Sam fixed his gaze on the glass door of Starbucks, waiting for any visual hints of Gaia Moore—the mass of blond hair still wet from a shower, the oversized army jacket with the massive black smudge on the right pocket, the filthy Nike sneakers. Or even just those aggressive "out-of-my-way" strides she called walking.

He'd run out of options. If she wouldn't return his phone calls or e-mails, he'd have to track her down. It was the only way, although attempting to corner Gaia was about as effective as cornering a deeply agitated grizzly.

But Sam was willing to risk injury at this point. It didn't matter that the last time he'd seen her, she'd pushed him aside and run out of her father's apartment, leaving him stranded—quite possibly for good. Nor did it matter that he'd decimated her trust in him with all his little white lies, idiotic tales to cover for those criminal errands Josh was forcing on him. It didn't even matter that the simple act of *seeing* Gaia had been strictly forbidden by the gutless assholes who threatened him daily by phone, too cowardly to even show their faces.

None of it mattered now.

Because of the letter.

Christ, how many weeks had passed from the time Gaia had sent her e-mail from Paris and the time Sam had received it? How much damage had been done? First, those dim-witted cops, Riley and Bernard, had confiscated his computer. Then, when Sam had finally been cleared of suspicion and his computer was returned, he'd gotten so many vicious e-mails from the faceless blackmailers that he'd simply stopped checking his mail. And he'd certainly stopped picking up the phone. How many more threats did he really need to hear?

But for some reason today, Sam had awoken feeling particularly brave (or was it just hopeless?)—and thank God for it, or he never would have checked his mail. He never would have known that he was the recipient of the one and only love letter ever written by Gaia Moore. A reluctant love letter, perhaps, but still, a sorely needed reminder of everything that was meant to be.

Gaia had almost convinced Sam in their last meeting that their relationship was an absolute impossibility; there were too many complications, too much emotional baggage, inevitable doom—not to mention violence, kidnappings, and brushes with death. But there, on his computer screen this morning, were

Gaia's own words, written only a matter of weeks before. And reading them, seeing her struggle beautifully to be naked and intimate with him in ways she usually avoided like bubonic plague, and of course the words *I love you. . .* all of it was a desperately needed shot of adrenaline. It brought Sam back to the simple reality that both he and Gaia had endured far too much not to end up together. Anything less would be unacceptably dark and tragic. Even for them—

Sam's heart froze.

She's here.

He hadn't even realized it: Gaia was standing at the register with an overstuffed duffel bag slung over her shoulder. It was almost as big as she was, but she managed it almost effortlessly.

Without thinking, Sam launched to his feet and sidled up next to her at the adjacent counter. Gaia took her coffee and stuffed a dollar into the makeshift tip jar, then let a river of sugar cascade into her cup. She didn't lift her head.

Does she know it's me?

"Uh. . . hi," he began with a cautious smile. He was worried he might startle her, until he remembered that hardly anything ever startled her.

Gaia turned to him. For the briefest instant her face seemed to tighten; it was as if her skin were stretched taut over those beautiful cheekbones. But her blue eyes were like ice. She blinked, then stared back down at her coffee.

Sam's insides squeezed painfully. He knew he shouldn't have expected her to collapse into his arms. But he wasn't going to give up. "Laundry day?" he asked, glancing at the bag.

The seconds ticked by in silence.

"What are you doing here?" she finally asked, lifting her coffee cup. She blew on the steamy black liquid, keeping her gaze pinned to it. Her voice was flat, lifeless.

"I. . . I have to talk to you," Sam breathed, leaning across the counter, desperately trying to regain eye contact. He searched for the hint of any emotion. There was none.

Gaia took a sip from the cup, then looked to the clock above the door. "Shit, I'm late," she mumbled.

Sam spoke to her turned cheek. "Gaia, look at me and talk. This is ridiculous."

"I'm late," she repeated—maybe to herself, maybe to him; Sam couldn't tell, and it didn't make a difference. Her reaction to him represented everything he'd been dreading: an utter coldness, an unfamiliar blank stare. Sam remembered the first time he'd ever seen her at the chess tables in Washington Square Park: that very first game, when he'd sat across from her and lost track of everything—the game, the rain—and fixated on the few light freckles, on the way the rain drenched her blond hair and dripped from her cheeks. She looked exactly as she had that day. Just as beautiful. . .

just as much of a stranger.

Gaia adjusted the bag on her hip and walked out onto Sixth Avenue with her coffee. Sam blew out a brief disheartened sigh and followed. She was already a few yards down the street by the time he got outside. He caught up and tried to keep pace with her brisk steps.

"What do you have in that bag?" he asked.

"It's just . . ." Her voice trailed off, and she increased her speed. "It's nothing. Stuff."

They flew down Cornelia Street. All the brownstones were beginning to blur in Sam's peripheral vision. Thoughts of that runaway train began to creep back into his psyche. *The brakes, Sam. Slam on the brakes.* He froze on Bleecker Street, hoping Gaia would stop with him. But she didn't. Of course she didn't.

"Jesus, will you stop?" he pleaded, swallowing all his pride for one brief moment.

Gaia turned her head back but kept her body moving forward at a steady pace. "I can't," she called back. "If I'm late to this class again, I'll get reamed. Sorry—"

"I got your letter," Sam interrupted.

It was not at all how he'd wanted to say it, like an announcement over a high school PA system, but he could think of nothing else that might cut through Gaia's icy veneer.

Gaia hesitated.

"I finally got my computer back. . . ," he added, "from

the shop." Sam nearly winced at having to throw in a white lie at this point, but he still hadn't told Gaia about the police and his near indictment for Mike's murder. That would mean telling her about Josh's "help" with the alibi, which could lead to Josh's terrorizing boss or *bosses*. . . and that could put Gaia in danger.

She stared at him.

"I barely remember writing it," she said, stone-faced. "I'd had a lot of wine." Gaia broke eye contact and looked down at the sidewalk. "It seems like such a long time ago."

"It wasn't," Sam said. He moved a few steps closer. "Gaia—"

"I'm sorry," she said, turning and flicking her finger over her eye. Was she wiping away a tear? Sam felt a bolt of optimism—coupled with shock. The odds of Gaia's crying were considerably low. Practically nonexistent. But maybe she was actually giving in to a feeling. Any feeling was a good start.

"Sorry? Why are you sorry?" Sam asked, taking a step closer. His heart lurched. Her eyes were definitely red and glazed with tears. She *was* crying. He couldn't believe it. Something must be very, very wrong. The nagging guilt he carried around with him at all times suddenly tripled.

"I'm. . . it's just—I'm not trying to be. . . ," she stammered with a catch in her throat.

"It's *okay*," Sam assured her. He had no idea what to

do. This outpouring and uncertainty were all so new, so disturbing. Without even realizing it, he found himself closing the gap between them, putting his arms around her, bringing her head to his chest and holding her tightly. She didn't resist. . . not exactly. But it was as if every part of her were willing his arms away from her waist. They were like two repelling magnets.

He pulled his arms away, knowing the moment offered him no other choice than to step back from her. And then they stood in silence, focusing on the smaller details of the sidewalk—the bright red canvas of a baby stroller, the tires of a parked car, looking anywhere but at each other.

"I better go," she said finally.

"Sure."

Sam thrust his hands into his pockets and looked away toward the street. He preferred not to watch Gaia walk away again. He'd experienced that enough already.

IT HAD BEEN A VERY LONG TIME since Ed Fargo had seen the tops of people's heads. As he hobbled down the hall, struggling on his crutches, he made sure to avoid everyone's glances—those stupid

patronizing smiles and "okay" signs. Instead he focused on the parts of the hall he'd never noticed before. There was a strip of black rubber that lined the top of the puke green lockers. There were wads of chewing gum that had probably been stuck atop those lockers for twenty years. Why hadn't he noticed back when he was walking? Had he *grown* since the last time he walked? He realized that quite possibly he had. He found himself literally looking down at a lot of his classmates.

He had only two goals, what with his bag dangling from his right hand, knocking against his crutch with every frustrating step.

1. Keep an eye out for Heather. The inevitable confrontation was fast approaching, and Ed would need to be prepared.

2. Find Gaia. She was the only one in that entire school who would treat Ed like he was Ed. No thumbs-up. No idiotic gawking. No congratulations. Just the usual banter. Business as usual. Ed needed somebody to swat him back to reality. And if there was one thing Gaia was good at, it was that.

Finally, Ed thought. He managed a grin—not an easy feat, considering the crutches were digging into his armpits and his legs felt like they were about to fall off. But there was Gaia, trying to stuff a huge bag into her locker as her books fell out on the floor. He took two giant strides, crashing into the lockers with his shoulders—and nearly toppling over—as he landed next to her.

"You are the person I needed to see," he grunted.

Gaia nodded, smiling tiredly. "Same here," she mumbled, finally cramming her bag into her locker and slamming it closed. "Say something nice, Fargo. I'm having a lousy life."

"Something nice, Fargo."

"You know, I should have seen that coming," Gaia muttered, but she laughed as she picked up the books that had fallen onto the floor. "If it's going to be something funny, then it should actually be funny. But I asked for something nice."

"You're the sister I never had?" he offered, with just a hint of sarcasm. It was more of a question than a statement.

Gaia rolled her eyes. "You *have* a sister." She cracked the locker back open and shoved the books back in, one at a time.

"Don't remind me," Ed grumbled. He placed his hand on the locker door just above Gaia's head, helping her to hold it firm as she slipped the last book back in.

"Thanks, I think I can handle it," she muttered as she slammed the door closed once again.

"Oh, right," he said, matching her tone. "Sorry, I keep forgetting you're a superhero."

Incredibly enough, his comment actually elicited

another smile. *Two for two,* Ed thought. Not bad for a Monday morning.

"Very funny," she said, turning to look up at him.

Suddenly the smile dropped from her face.

Ed frowned. "What's wrong?"

But Gaia didn't answer. Instead she just stared at Ed as if he were a specimen from some distant galaxy.

"What's. . . the. . . problem?" he repeated slowly, in case she might have missed some part of the question. He tried to muster a little laugh again. But he was starting to feel a nervous twitch in his stomach.

"Nothing," she replied finally. She turned away.

"What?" he pressed. "Do I have pen on my face or something?"

"I have to go," she said. Her voice took on an edge. She stared up at him again, her eyes darting from point to point on Ed's face. "I'm late for MacGregor."

Now he was officially uncomfortable. "So what? I am, too."

"Well, I don't want to flunk the class, so . . ." Gaia turned to leave, but he stuck out his left crutch to hold her up.

"Hey. What happened to 'say something nice'?"

He searched her face, trying to understand her bizarre, sudden shift in personality—although he knew he shouldn't have been surprised. She'd been switching personalities a lot lately, going from sour and ornery one moment to mysteriously blissful the next. But far more disturbing was that she had stopped being completely honest at all times. Gaia Moore's unflinching honesty, more than anything—even more than the ass kicking and the Amazonian beauty—was what separated Gaia from pretty much every other human being on the planet.

"I'll—I'll. . . try to find you at lunch," she stammered, running her hand through her hair and avoiding eye contact. "*Later*, okay?"

Well. There was clearly no point in trying to understand what was going on here. All he knew was that he was starting to feel awfully shitty. Did this have something to do with his being out of the chair? Was that what was making her so distant?

No. Not Gaia. How could *she* be thrown by seeing him on his feet? She'd seen right past his chair, so why the hell wouldn't she be able to see past his crutches? There was some undeniable energy passing between them, but he couldn't tell if it was positively charged or negatively charged. Gaia wasn't giving him any clues. He'd never had to *ask* for clues before.

"Gaia," he said, searching for recognition in her eyes. "It's *me. Ed.* You know, *Ed.* The dude in the wheelchair? Same guy."

But Gaia had no response.

GAIA'S HEAD WAS SPINNING. SHE

found she was royally pissed off, and she had no idea

Queen Bitch to the Rescue

why. All she knew was that her anger was directed at Ed, and Ed was really the only reason she'd even bothered to come to school before heading over to the Mosses' house. It made no sense.

Maybe there were just too many thoughts crowding her brain at the same time. There was the horrific encounter with Sam. She didn't want to deal with that. Couldn't think about it now. There was always the absence of her dad. *Avoid that thought at all costs.* There was her new chaotic and absurd emotional status to consider (coupled with sleeplessness), a condition referred to commonly as insanity. That couldn't help.

Was it just the crutches? She hadn't expected the crutches. She hadn't even seen Ed since the day he'd saved her ass in the park. But now, frozen in this goddamn hall, looking up at Ed, face-to-face . . .

First of all, just looking *up* at Ed was undeniably bizarre. Gaia wasn't proud of herself for noticing this. She was ashamed—and that's when she realized she had been mistaken. Her anger wasn't directed at Ed. It was directed at herself. Because Ed *wasn't* Ed. Of course he was Ed, but he was. . . tall. And he was so much closer. There was something disturbing about being face-to-face, without the chair between them. This Ed just didn't feel as. . . safe.

So she had to leave. She turned—and nearly slammed into Heather Gannis, whose beautiful porcelain face was shriveled like a prune, framed by that shiny dark hair in a portrait of sheer rage. *Perfect,* Gaia thought. Queen bitch to the rescue. Never once had she ever imagined she'd be happy to see Heather, but then, today was bringing a lot of unexpected changes. She should just roll with it.

"Excuse me," Heather spat.

Gaia smiled. "You're excused," she answered calmly.

Heather took a step back, gesturing with an angry thrust of her arms toward the hall as if to say, "Be my guest."

Good. Now Gaia was free. She made her way down the hall, making sure not to look back. She tried to force a wave of numbness to take over, but it was no use. The feelings were piling up like cars in a highway tractor-trailer disaster—crashing into her without any warning, flipping her upside down, and burying her under the weight of each new collision. And she felt everything.

HEATHER STARED AT ED FOR AS LONG

as she could without speaking. Her body was on fire.

Miracle of Miracles

Those goddamn crutches. Why did he have to do it? Why couldn't he have sat in the wheelchair just a little longer? She wanted to make him squirm. She wanted to make him feel like shit. Basically, she wanted to hurt him the way he'd hurt her. If that were even possible.

Here he was, not only walking—not only breaking his vow of secrecy to her and pretty much ruining any chance she ever had of seeing that money—he was talking with Gaia. Intimately.

"You want to tell me what that was about?" she demanded.

Ed stared at the floor, looking very much like a dog with its tail between its legs. But that wasn't the look she was going for. She was going for pain.

Sharp sensations needled the base of Heather's stomach. She hadn't spoken to Ed in almost a week. For all she knew, Ed and Gaia had fallen right into bed, all turned on by Ed's lifesaving heroics in the park. Of course. Gaia "Man-eater" Moore always got what she wanted or, rather, *who* she wanted. After all, Ed could make himself *walk* for Gaia. Miracle of miracles. For Heather. . . he couldn't even keep his mouth shut.

"I don't know what that was about," Ed finally

muttered.

He's still thinking about her. Heather's jaw tightened. He didn't even seem aware that his actual girlfriend was standing right in front of him.

"Oh, I'm sorry," Heather said with a big, phony smile, her voice dripping with sarcasm. "Was that a lover's quarrel? Did you want to go after her? You might as well, Ed. Your walking in public seems to be improving."

Ed flinched. *There* was the pain she was trying to bring. "Not here, Heather," he whispered. "Okay? Not now."

"Oh, are you too busy now?" Heather asked, the icy smile frozen in place. "When should I make an appointment, Ed? Can I book something between your walks with Gaia?"

Suddenly Heather heard titters from behind her. When she turned around, she saw Carrie Longman and Tina Lynch—gaping at her, trying not to laugh, hands cupped around their mouths. Well. This was just what she needed. There was apparently no finer entertainment for her friends than watching her life fall apart. But she couldn't deal with them now.

"We need to talk, Ed," she hissed, backing away from him. "We need to talk *tonight.*"

"I *know,*" Ed replied shakily. "I want to talk. I really am sorry, Heather, you have to believe me." He looked stricken. "Let me call you tonight. We'll go somewhere where we can really talk, okay? We'll have dinner."

Heather looked into Ed's eyes. For the briefest instant she felt a twinge of guilt. She suddenly realized that she was looking *up* to see Ed's eyes. Her heart lurched, and she almost smiled—sparked simply by the change in their physical orientation. But the memories of his past sweetness only led her back to his present betrayal. A wave of fresh anger followed.

"That better not be another lie," she warned. "You'd better call me tonight, Ed."

"I will," he assured her.

"You better not let me down," she whispered, almost mouthing the words for fear her friends would hear. "Do *not* let me down again."

I'm confused. This morning before school, "crutching" my way down the street, trying not to get knocked over or trampled on, there was one thing I was sure of: I couldn't stand the invisibility. I felt like a goddamn human turnstile, like I was just this little obstacle between point *A* and point *B*, and all anyone had to do was push right through me.

But when I hobbled into school this morning. . . it was like I was hobbling onto the red carpet at the Oscars. No longer a turnstile, I was now a superstar. And it made me sick to my stomach. It left me begging for invisibility. Go figure.

Everyone (and I mean that literally) seems to have gotten wind of my new and improved walking capabilities. And if I have to look at one more condescending congratulatory smile or one more "you *go*, ex-cripple!" thumbs-up, I swear to God, I'm going to cripple one of *them*.

It's like they're all saying, "Ed! Where have you been? Welcome back to the world of the living!" All I want to do is scream in their faces, "I'm not back from the *dead*, you asshole!" Was I such a pathetic loser when I was in the chair? It's degrading.

I'm the exact same guy, you idiots. In a chair, on crutches, on my feet.

Same guy.

She didn't
want to
fight the
emotion. She

gunshots

wanted to
drink it in,
thirstily,
like wine.

BERLIN WAS THE LAST PLACE ON earth Tom wanted to be right now—although any place other than home with Gaia would have felt equally as torturous. She could only hate him at this point. There was no doubt of that. After all his promises. . . to simply disappear again, leaving nothing but a cursory note, it must have appeared to be his all-time low.

Porcelain Angel

Appeared? It *was* his all-time low.

Since the moment he and Gaia set foot in their Mercer Street apartment, Tom had begun to entertain one notion far more seriously than ever before: Maybe he had finally done enough for his country. Maybe it was time for Enigma to disappear and for Tom Moore to risk the consequences.

But the agency had given him no choice. Not when Gaia's safety was at stake. If there truly was a leak in Loki's organization and the agency wanted Tom in Berlin as the contact, that's where he would be. He'd be there even if they *didn't* want him as the contact. If this informant knew anything about Loki's inevitable plans and how they might involve Gaia, Tom wanted to hear them firsthand.

He wouldn't risk any possible misinterpretation. No one on this earth was more qualified to interpret

Loki's sadistic logic than his own twin. Yes, Tom was where he needed to be: sitting on a park bench in the public square just beyond the Brandenburg Gate.

The square was filled with loud tourists who fired off photo after photo of the imposing gate, with its massive pillars and the triumphant sculpture of a four-horse-driven chariot at its peak—the Quadriga. The more people, the better, as far as he was concerned. He could melt into the crowd here. It had been a long time since Tom had been in Berlin. He shivered. He'd forgotten how cold it could get. Cold and foggy.

The informant refused to give any identifying information. His gender was just about the only thing the Agency knew about him. He was obviously skittish. Who wouldn't be after choosing to betray Loki? That was something akin to a self-imposed death sentence. So Tom had no idea who or what to look for. The informant had only said that Tom would know when the time was right.

It felt like hours had passed before a young girl approached him at the park bench. She was selling German chocolate bars from a cardboard box. Tom smiled. She had long blond hair, and she couldn't have been more than ten years old. She was wearing a white dress, like a porcelain angel. She was utterly adorable. Until she came closer.

Her eyes. . . from a distance Tom could have sworn

they were blue, but when she stepped closer, they were so dark, they appeared nearly black.

"Is your name Tom?" the little girl asked with a German accent.

"Yes, it is," Tom replied. "What's your name?"

"My name is Gaia," she said. "And I'm going to die."

Tom stiffened. There was a split second of uncomprehending, paralyzing shock—and then gunshots were echoing through the square, one after the other, seemingly coming from every angle.

This is an ambush. I've been set up.

Tom screamed for the crowd to drop to the ground, to no avail. Panicked tourists fell over each other in terror. Tom pounced on the little girl, knocking her to the ground, desperately trying to protect her from the spray of bullets. The shots seemed infinite. The screams were deafening, melding together into a high-pitched screech that was gouging Tom's eardrums. Flashbulbs blinded his eyes, and the cold white ground was like ice, painful to the skin and wet. Had it begun to rain?

And then, very abruptly, the gunfire ceased.

Tom lifted himself off the girl to make sure she was unharmed.

"Oh my God," he said.

He wasn't wet from rain. He was wet from her blood.

"Dad?" she moaned, blood trickling from her mouth and soaking through her white dress. "Why did you leave me? How could you leave me again?"

Tom's breathing became short and forced. He was beginning to hyperventilate. He couldn't speak. He couldn't even scream. The sound of his breath echoed through his head, over and over. Getting louder and louder—

He jerked upright.

It was a dream.

The square was gone, as was the blood and the girl.

He was soaked in his own sweat in his hotel in Berlin. The sun through the window was blinding. The screech of the terrorized crowd was now a horrible noise blasting from the hotel alarm clock. Tom slammed it off and ripped the wet sheet from his body, then jumped out of bed. He didn't wait to collect himself from his horrible nightmare. Instead he dropped into the chair of the hotel desk and tore a piece of notepaper from the pad. He was still gasping for air.

Dearest Gaia,

You can't read this, but I have to write it. I swear to you I'll be back as quickly as I can. If it can be a day, it will be a day. I have not abandoned you, Gaia. Some part of you knows this, I'm sure of it. Just as I'm sure some part of you despises me. Wait for me, Gaia. Please. And protect yourself. Not just your body, but your heart and your mind, too. Your sanity can protect you. And then I'll be home. I promise.

Tom crumpled the note and stuffed it in his briefcase. He walked to the window and stared down at the stark Berlin streets. He had no faith whatsoever in premonitions. He was a pure pragmatist. But the dream had shaken him to such an extent that he actually found himself believing for a split second that he'd been given a horrible glimpse of future events.

So he did all he could do. He prayed that he was wrong.

"SHE'S HERE! SHE'S HERE, SHE'S here!" Mrs. Moss greeted Gaia with a warm embrace that quickly turned into a suffocating bear hug.

Gaia watched over Mrs. Moss's shoulder as the rest of the family gathered in the foyer to greet her, each of them with bright grins of anticipation. The next world war had just ended, and this was her long-awaited homecoming. She had just entered some fantasyland—one so alien, she could hardly process it. But then, fantasyland was just another term for Central Park West: the Victorian colored glass chandeliers, the varnished blond wood floors, and those elegant but funky antiques that only Mrs. Moss could have found.

And then there was the family. It was so strange; when Gaia had first come to New York, she hated "the beautiful people"—the happy wanderers who walked the city without a care in the world other than their next shopping journey. Had she seen any member of the Moss clan at that time, all would have certainly fallen into that category. But now she could appreciate their beauty. Just as she had appreciated Mary's.

They lined up in a row to hug Gaia. First came Mr. Moss—who was sturdy and somewhat nondescript, with brown hair and brown eyes and a deep comforting smile. Then came Mary's oldest brother, Brendan, the NYU student—and Sam's former suite mate.

Gaia held her breath. A burst of adrenaline coursed through her veins. She'd been expecting that seeing Brendan would dredge up all the recent Sam-related horror and misery. A small part of her also half expected him to lash at her; she knew he was no great fan of Sam's. But miraculously, nothing happened. He just offered her the same melancholy smile as his father had. The apartment was a fortress, a magical fortress that seemed to keep the outside world at bay.

Then came Mary's brother Paul, whom Gaia suddenly remembered—with crimson-faced embarrassment as he hugged her—as "the cute one." Paul had much more in common with Mary and her mom physically, with the exception of course of the quarter inch of reddish blond stubble on his chin. But his shaggy hair was a shade of red bordering on blond, and his eyes were the exact same shade of bright blue.

The next few minutes passed in a blur. Gaia felt like she was being carried along by a wonderful, warm, and enveloping current; she was powerless to do anything but watch, to let the experience wash over her. The family immediately ushered her into the dining room and sat her down for dinner. The scent of "real" food wafted in from the kitchen as Olga, the family cook, brought in a platter of roast chicken. Gaia suddenly realized she was starving. After weeks of pizza and chili dogs and doughnuts, she was worried that she'd grab the chicken and start ripping it from the bone with her teeth, like some homeless savage wild child who'd been raised by wolves and was attempting her first "civilized" dinner. Olga brought the tray to Gaia's left and offered her chicken. Gaia took only one piece even though she wanted ten.

"Take more, dear," Olga said. "You look hungry."

Gaia flashed a self-effacing smile. "You're right." She took another piece. "Thank you."

"I always forget that you speak Russian," Mrs. Moss marveled as she took some chicken.

"I'm sorry?" Gaia asked.

"Russian," Mrs. Moss repeated. "You and Olga were just speaking Russian."

Gaia looked up at Olga in surprise. Olga flashed a warm smile. *Whoa*, Gaia thought. She really *was* out of it. They were speaking Russian, and she hadn't even noticed.

"Do you speak any other languages?" Paul asked.

"A few," Gaia said casually.

Then Mrs. Moss said something to Gaia in Dutch. Gaia shrugged and smiled as if Mrs. Moss had stumped her. Of course she knew exactly what was said; she was just too embarrassed to respond to it.

We're so happy to have you here.

"We're so happy to have you here!" Paul stated triumphantly.

Gaia lowered her eyes. Her face felt hot. She was blushing. She couldn't remember the last time she had felt so bewildered and happy at the same time, as if she were five years old. But she didn't want to fight the emotion. She wanted to drink it in, thirstily, like wine.

"Chill, bro," Brendan joked. "Save it for the bonus round." He glanced at Gaia. "You'll have to excuse my brother, Gaia. He doesn't get out much."

"Real funny," Paul replied with a smile.

An awkward beat passed.

Gaia looked up and saw that Mr. and Mrs. Moss weren't smiling at all. Maybe there was a little too much truth to that statement. Mrs. Moss had said that Paul was living at home instead of at his Columbia dorm and that she could hear him crying at night behind his closed door. And when Gaia turned to Paul again, there was still a smile on his face—but there was undoubtedly something else behind it. A sadness in his eyes. Somebody would have to look closely to see it, but Gaia had done just that. And seeing that unbearable emptiness just beyond his functional surface was very much like having a mirror on the other side of the dining table.

"Well, I'm going out *tonight*," Paul muttered after a moment.

"Oh, yeah, that's right," Brendan said. "Gaia, there's a Fearless show at CBGB's tonight. You've got to come with us."

"Sure," she agreed absently, her mind drifting into the past. "God, I haven't been to a Fearless show since Mary and I—"

She cut herself off instantly. Mary's name had not been mentioned once. Sitting in the sudden awkward silence, Gaia wondered if she'd just made a massive error—perhaps the biggest error a person could make in the Moss household.

"Gaia," Mrs. Moss said gently, as if reading her mind, "we talk about her all the time. We talk about her as often as possible, and you should feel free to do the same. I know you loved her as much as we did. As

60

much as we *do*."

Gaia nodded and swallowed, then allowed herself a small sigh of relief. Talking about Mary was something Gaia would have never allowed herself to do alone. But in a way, that was what Mary's gift had always been to her: the chance to do something she never would have done alone—whether it was going to a Fearless show, wearing a tight red dress, playing a game of truth or dare, or just listening to someone else's problems instead of dwelling on her own.

"I did," Gaia said, just barely holding off another wave of emotion. "I mean, I do. But my point is this," she announced, squelching every ounce of her sadness. She replaced her wimpy self-pitying tone with something bold and absurdly declamatory. "Tonight. . . I must *rock*."

Everybody stared at her.

Then Paul laughed. So did Brendan. Mrs. Moss cracked a puzzled smile.

It was an unquestionably stupid thing to say, but somehow Gaia knew that Paul would think it was funny. And that was precisely why she had said it. If she could make a member of the Moss family laugh, then she knew she was doing something worthwhile.

From: smoon@alloymail.com
To: gaia13@alloymail.com
Time: 6:48 P.M.
Re: The truth

Gaia,

I hated what happened this morning. It hurt more than you can imagine. But I know it's my fault. Because you don't trust me. And why should you? I've been lying to you, and I know you can tell. But I've only been lying to protect you. You have to believe that.

I'm in real trouble, Gaia. And I think you may be, too

<DELETE>

Gaia,

I have to see you tonight. I know you think I'm a liar, but there's so much you don't know. I want to tell you everything. I need to tell you. I'm being blackmailed, and I'm not even sure who is doing it. Josh is working for them, and now I'm working for him. I don't even know if I'm going to come out of this

<DELETE>

Gaia,

 I have to put an end to all of this, and I
have to tell you everything. You have to meet
me tonight. But if I have to leave, it's only
because they can't see us together. If they see
us together, you could be

<DELETE>

From: smoon@alloymail.com
To: gaia13@alloymail.com
Time: 7:03 P.M.
Re: Tonight

Gaia,

 I'm sorry about this morning. I shouldn't
have surprised you like that. It was the wrong
choice. Please agree to see me tonight. Say you
will, even if you don't want to. It's urgent.
And I wouldn't say that if it weren't true. I
need to see you. Please write back as soon as
you get this. I've tried calling you, and
there's no answer. I don't know where you are,
and I worry about you.

I love you.

Sam

For the first
time in weeks,
he felt he could
safely unload the
enormous **bullshit**
guilt
he'd been **smiles**
carrying with
him. He'd drop
it like a sack
of bricks.

"DELIVERY!"

Josh Kendall now barged into Sam's room at will. Sam jumped slightly but managed to click on the send command before Josh had a chance to see what he was doing. Not

Calculated Risk

that it particularly mattered if Sam were caught. Whatever Josh missed, somebody else was sure to see. Sam now operated on the principle of "calculated risk." It was something he'd learned from chess.

At least there was an upside to the whole situation: he was able to put his long-standing paranoia to rest. He no longer had to wonder if "they" were watching his every move. He knew now that they were. He accepted it as just another part of his life—like homework, or labs, or classes. That was half the reason he'd been careful not to mention any specifics in his e-mail to Gaia. The other half was that he didn't want to worry her until he could explain everything face-to-face.

Josh exhaled with a grin. He dropped yet another brown paper package on Sam's clothing-covered bed.

"Shit," he said. "This has got to be delivered by six-thirty, Sammy, so you better get going now."

Sam turned to Josh, his jaw tightly set. He made no attempt to mask his hatred. There was no point.

Josh clapped in front of Sam's nose like some psychotic inspirational football coach.

"Come on, Sammy, let's move, *move.*"

Sam shot out of his chair, knocking his shoulder into Josh's chin as he stood up. Another calculated risk—and well worth it. Josh's head snapped back, and his features contorted as he winced with pain.

"Hey, are you all right?" Sam asked, locking eyes with him. "You should be more careful around me. I can be really clumsy."

Josh massaged his jaw and shook his head slowly. He met Sam's gaze with that Teflon smile still pasted back onto his perfect, handsome, evil face.

"Sam," he said, oozing with condescension, "the thing you *don't* want to do now is get cocky. That would be astronomically stupid."

"I don't know what you mean," Sam replied as he picked up the package.

"We're almost there, Sam," Josh said. "We're so close. So what I strongly suggest you do. . . is *behave.*"

Sam was already standing at the doorway of his room. "Josh," he said, holding up the package, "I've got a *delivery,* man. You're going to make me *late.*" Then he turned away and slammed the door behind him.

ED STARED AT THE PHONE AS IF it had radioactive properties. As if it might burn through his hand if he actually picked up the receiver. He considered some of the things he'd rather do than call Heather and arrange a dinner for the sole purpose of letting her bawl him out.

Kinder, Gentler Heather

Would I rather be pelted with hot coals?

Check.

Would I rather have earphones taped to my head that would play nothing but Barry Manilow and Yanni twenty-four hours a day?

Check.

Would I rather be repeatedly hit on the head with a tire iron?

Actually, that would hurt. Good. Finally he had found something worse than calling Heather. So now he could do it. Besides, he knew that a dinner meeting—alone, face-to-face but in a public setting so as to avoid any violence or major freak-outs—was the only possible way to move past all the lies. To move past the miscommunication. And most important, to move past the money. There was no way to mend their relationship without calling.

Ed glanced around his empty kitchen. For a second he thought about pulling out his wheelchair just so he could sit and gather his strength. Nah. Better just to stand, to savor every painful moment. He leaned against the wall on his crutches, then placed the phone to his ear and slowly dialed her number.

After two rings somebody picked up.

"Hello?"

Heather's voice was much warmer than Ed had expected. It was more than warm; it was almost. . . *sprightly.*

"Hey," he said. "It's me."

"I'm sorry, who is this? Is this Ed?"

Shit. It wasn't Heather. It was her mom. Why did they have to sound so much alike on the phone? Ed drew in a deep breath. "Yes, it is," he said, adding as much polite good cheer as he could muster. "How are you, Mrs. Gannis?"

"Well, Ed, I'm doing great. We're all doing *great.*"

Ed knew that Mrs. Gannis had the tendency to accentuate the positive when in public—in other words, to be a complete phony. They were not doing great. They were doing terribly. But pretensions of flawlessness probably went back for generations in the Gannis family. I was a little sad to think of centuries of bullshit smiles and fake laughter.

"Well, I'm glad to hear it," Ed said, humoring her (and postponing the inevitable). "I was worried about you guys."

"Oh, Ed, there's no need to worry," she assured

him. "Phoebe's back home from the center, and she's doing great. And Mr. Gannis just landed a fantastic new job!"

Ed blinked. Wow. Apparently Mrs. Gannis wasn't just pouring on the joy for Ed's sake. Heather certainly hadn't mentioned anything about her dad's getting a new job. But this was fantastic news. If Mr. Gannis was making money of his own again, then Heather wouldn't need the cash from Ed's settlement so badly. That would mean that Ed hadn't destroyed Heather's life by taking those steps in public. And that would mean maybe, just maybe, that Heather wouldn't have to hate Ed's guts. Could he see a light at the end of the proverbial tunnel?

"Uh. . . that's great news, Mrs. Gannis!" he said. "I had no idea."

"Yes, well. We certainly needed some good news in this house."

"Yeah," Ed agreed. "Is Heather home?"

"She sure is, Ed. Hold on one second."

Ed sat back in his bed. His heart rate finally began to slow, and his chest began to expand more comfortably. For the first time in weeks he felt he could safely unload the enormous guilt he'd been carrying with him. He'd drop it like a sack of bricks. The state of Heather's family no longer depended entirely on his settlement. His walking was no longer perversely tied to Heather's survival. He was neither the hero nor the goat. He was just Ed again—plain old Ed. Maybe now he and Heather could just concentrate on salvaging their critically damaged relationship. Maybe this phone call wasn't going to be such a nightmare after all.

"Hello?" Heather asked.

"Hey!" Ed blurted out. "Why didn't you tell me about your dad and Phoebe?"

There was dead silence on the phone.

"Could you have waited any longer to call me?" she mumbled after a few seconds.

Ed scowled. So much for a kinder, gentler Heather. Apparently Heather's mood from the afternoon had stayed fully intact. Or gotten worse. He didn't understand it. Maybe she was suffering from an unspecified illness.

"I just. . . finished my physical therapy," Ed lied. "But I—"

"Where are we going to dinner?" Heather snapped.

Ed's pulse returned to high speed. "I. . . thought I'd pick you up."

"Fine."

"I'm. . . on my way."

"Fine." One small click and the line was dead.

Ed dropped the phone on the hook. He was too confused to do anything but stand there and stare into space. But suddenly being repeatedly hit on the head with a tire iron didn't seem so bad.

MEMO

To: L
From: J
Date: February 26
File: 776250
Subject: Messenger

Messenger is in hand but showing signs of rebellion. Please advise.

MEMO

To: J
From: L
Date: February 26
File: 776250
Subject: Messenger

Our potential leak is rebellion enough. Project is becoming time sensitive. Increase pressure to messenger. The warning stage has passed. Execute scare tactics.

From: gaia13@alloymail.com
To: smoon@alloymail.com
Time: 8:20 P.M.
Re: Tonight

Sam,

You don't need to worry about me. I'm fine.
I'm just staying with the Moss family for a
while, and then I'll see. . .

I'm sorry about this morning, too. Don't
take it the wrong way. I've just got this little crying problem right now. Nothing to be
concerned about. It will pass, I'm sure.

I can't see you tonight. I've got plans. But
I'll try to make contact tomorrow. If I can.

—G

Suddenly she
wished she were
far away—back on
the streets
of **opposite**
Alphabet
City, **effect**
someplace where
she inflicted
pain instead of
experiencing it.

"YOU LOOK DIFFERENT," PAUL MOSS said, examining Gaia from the doorway of Mary's room. "What did you do?"

Gaia shrugged, staring at herself in the little mirror perched on Mary's bureau. "Nothing. I put on some fatigues," she said. "Going to CBGB's is like going into battle. The mosh pit can get pretty ferocious."

Paul laughed. "Yeah, I guess that's true." He took a step forward, then suddenly froze. He sniffed the air. "God, it really smells like her in here."

Gaia's body tensed. The smile dropped from Paul's face. She quickly looked away, feeling her throat begin to tighten. She'd noticed the smell, too. And everything else. All of Mary's perfume was still lined up on top of the bureau. Her jewelry was still strung along the corners of the mirror. Her clothes were still hung up in the closet. (Of course, if she really had been alive, every piece of clothing in that closet would have been strewn out across the room.) Even her computer was still sitting on her desk.

Her parents must have had a reason for leaving the room intact. They must have felt that getting rid of the room would be like getting rid of Mary. Gaia would have handled the situation differently. She would have torn that room to shreds the minute Mary was gone. She would have turned it into a giant closet, or a darkroom, or a gym. Because she could see Mary behind her, listening to her bitch, red hair wrapped up in a giant bun on her head, pinned in place by takeout chopsticks. . .

"I'm sorry," Paul whispered.

"Me too," Gaia breathed, her voice catching. She looked back at Paul, who was still frozen at one step into the room. "Do you want to come in?" she asked, not quite sure what was holding him back.

"I don't come in here," Paul mumbled.

Nice. Chalk up some more idiot points. Gaia slapped her hand on her forehead and ran it back through her hair. "I'm sorry," she said. "I understand. I'm such a moron—"

"No, Gaia, it's fine," Paul assured her, waving his hands and giving her a warm smile. "It's not a big deal. It's . . ." Paul looked around the room slowly and then back at Gaia. "I don't know, when I walk in here, it feels like she should just be here. Like she should be standing right where you're standing . . ."

"Yeah," Gaia agreed. Suddenly she wished she were far away—back on the streets of Alphabet City, someplace where she inflicted pain instead of experienced it. "You're right. . . ."

"No, no, no," Paul said. "It's *fine,* Gaia, please. Relax."

Gaia stood there, immobilized. She couldn't think of any aspect of this scenario that wasn't awkward.

How could she possibly relax? What did she know about families and brothers? What did she know about grieving with *other people?* Next to nothing. Since the age of twelve Gaia had only grieved alone— for her mother, for her disappearing father, even for Mary. It was the only way Gaia knew how to cope. All she wanted was to take Paul's mind off his sadness, more even than she wanted to forget her own. But everything she said or did was only having the opposite effect. The mere fact of her being in Mary's room seemed only to be making things worse.

"Paul," she said, knowing no other approach but the direct one. "Maybe I shouldn't be here. I mean, there are a lot of other places I could—"

"What?" Paul interrupted. "What are you talking about? You just got here."

"I know, but—"

"Gaia . . ." He walked into the room and sat down on Mary's bed. She could see his features tightening, see the way he fought his discomfort with every movement. "It's like I said at dinner. We want you to be here. I mean, we're all getting a little sick of just talking to each other, anyway."

Gaia let out a small laugh. "You sound just like her."

Of course, this remark just led to another depressing and awkward silence. She racked her brain for a way to change the mood. What would she have done for herself? What would she have done if she were alone? That was really her only frame of reference.

"Okay, here's what I think," she said, sitting down on the bed. "I think when one of us gets too sad, we should just tell the other, and then we should immediately go do something completely random."

The words came from nowhere; Gaia was simply listening to herself speak. She couldn't believe how frank and presumptuous she was being. She'd made no mention of her own existential woes before this point. And it wasn't as if Paul had announced his depression or even made any attempt to share it with her. She barely knew him.

But she knew they were connected. Mary connected them.

"Sounds good," he said, catching Gaia off guard with his own frankness. "When do we start?"

Gaia breathed an internal sigh of relief. For some reason, her potentially ludicrous suggestion had made as much sense to Paul as it did to her. But when she thought about it, she knew why it had made so much sense to them both: it was exactly what Mary would have done.

"Uh. . . we can start now?" she offered.

"Okay," Paul agreed. He took a long, thoughtful pause before locking eyes with Gaia. "Actually. . . I think I'm okay right now."

Gaia took her own moment of self-examination

before she spoke. "Yeah," she concluded with the slightest hint of a smile. "Me too."

HEATHER WAITED FOR ED TO speak—keeping her eyes fixed in front of her, gazing down Houston Street at the remnants of the sunset. She tried to walk as slowly as possible so that he could keep up on his crutches, but her desire to stomp was difficult to suppress. They'd walked for blocks, and he still hadn't said a word. Not one apology, not one "I love you." With each block she felt smaller and more humiliated. And angrier Definitely angrier.

"Well, where are we going to dinner?" she forced herself to ask. She'd spent a fair amount of time getting dressed up for the evening.

"Um . . ." He obviously hadn't even planned a place. "Without that big settlement, I was thinking more along the lines of falafel."

Heather stopped their walk. "Falafel?" she spat.

"A joke," Ed said, with a pathetic smirk forming in the corner of his mouth. "Remember jokes?"

"It's not funny," Heather replied. She couldn't have imagined a worse joke for Ed to pick.

"I'm sorry," Ed said. At least he'd finally said it.

"Why don't we just walk until we find a place? I'm trying to walk as much as possible."

Heather's face darkened. She scrutinized his features, searching for any hint of regret or remorse for having brought up the walking once again—but she didn't see a thing. Incredible. He didn't even realize that he was rubbing his broken promise in her face. He was *that* clueless. It was pretty disturbing, actually. Heather had always thought of Ed as a very bright guy. But maybe he'd left his brains wherever he'd dumped his wheelchair.

"What?" Ed asked.

She shrugged and kept walking. "Nothing."

"You know what, Heather?" he said with a grunt, plodding on his crutches. "I thought maybe you'd be less angry at me since your dad got a job—"

"It's not about money, Ed!" Heather snapped, stopping cold again. "This isn't about that at all, all right? It's about breaking promises."

"*Okay, okay,*" Ed whispered, glancing furtively from side to side to make sure no passersby could hear them. "Will you calm down? I've told you how sorry I am. I don't know what else I can do, Heather. There was a slight *situation,* you know? Life-and-death-type stuff? I just reacted. I barely even knew I was walking."

"Of course," Heather hissed, laughing spitefully. "Gaia Moore! The damsel in distress! How could she possibly have saved herself?"

Ed groaned. "She's my *friend,* Heather. I thought she was going to *die,* for chrissake."

"Yeah, well, she didn't seem so concerned about *my* life when she let me stroll right into the park, knowing I was going to get slashed. Or have you forgotten about that, too?"

It was funny: until that very moment, Heather hadn't even realized that her current slew of problems had completely overshadowed a whole batch of prior resentments. When her sister was still trying to recover from anorexia and her family was just barely recovering from near bankruptcy, Heather hardly had time to think about all the ways Gaia Moore had tried to hurt her. But now it was all coming back in a flood of righteous anger: the way Gaia had stolen Sam from her (not that they were right for each other, but that wasn't the point). . . but mostly the way Gaia had let her walk right into a situation that could have gotten her killed.

Nothing would ever make her forget that attack in Washington Square. Nothing. She easily could have died, and if she had, it would have been for one reason and one reason only: Gaia Moore was a bitch who only cared about herself. Gaia couldn't have cared less if Heather lived or died that night, so if Ed thought that saving Gaia from her own pathetic and violent life was going to be a good enough reason to betray Heather, he'd better think again.

"I didn't forget my promise," he insisted quietly. "I tried to keep the promise. I even made Gaia keep my secret. How was I supposed to know someone else would see me and spread it all over school?"

"You shouldn't have to know, Ed!" Heather shouted. "Because you should have been with *me,* not with *her.*"

"What?"

Heather slapped her hands down to her sides, and her entire body froze on the corner of Houston and Sullivan. And then her mouth took over. "Wake up, Ed! This isn't just about betraying me. It's about *whom* you betrayed me for. Note my correct usage of 'whom.' Because I'm not an idiot, Ed. I'm not a blind idiot. You're in love with her. Do you think I'm so narcissistic that I haven't seen that?"

"Heather—"

"And I don't even know how you feel about me, Ed. I really don't. I mean, you can't really trust me if you still blame me."

Ed paused. He blinked several times rapidly, glaring at her in the fading sunlight. His face seemed to go pale. "For what?" he demanded.

"The *accident,* Ed," she said. And until the words were out there, dangling between them like a wrecking ball, she hadn't even realized she was going to bring it up. But she had lost control. She was too upset to think rationally. "Don't pretend you don't know what I'm talking about. I know you still blame me; we just don't talk about it. It's just buried there, right under the surface, like this rotting corpse stinking up our entire relationship." Her throat was so tight, she could barely finish. "If you don't know that by now, that's your problem, not mine."

She sniffed violently and wiped her face—and to her surprise, her hand came back wet. She hadn't even realized she was crying. Maybe she should just quit while she was ahead and get the hell away from him. After all, she'd pretty much said everything she had to say. And a lot of things she hadn't wanted to say. Now she just wanted to go home.

Ed's expression was oddly serious and resigned. "Nothing you just said was true," he stated.

"I'm out of here," she said, nearly whispering—not for dramatic effect, only out of weakness.

"I'll take you." Ed reached from his crutch to take Heather's hand.

"Don't," she said, shrinking away from him. And then, before she even knew it, she was sprinting east down Houston Street—toward the night that was fast approaching.

You'd think after all these months, I would have figured out what the hell goes on in the mind of Gaia Moore, but this morning proved once again that I have absolutely no clue.

I mean, sure, there are those days when she brings new meaning to the word *bitchy*, but I'm used to that. I know what that looks like. But that has nothing to do with what was going on this morning.

I've played the whole thing over so many times, and I still cannot figure out what I said to piss her off. I wasn't talking about Heather—that always pisses her off. I wasn't joking about her wardrobe—that's a great way to get her all riled up. Was it about what happened in the park? She hates it when I try to be the hero. But I don't think so. She was grateful for that day. I know she was.

Unless it did have something to do with the crutches. They

were really the only thing that
made this morning different
from any other morning. Maybe
she was just pissed to find out
I was taller than she was—
which, I must admit, I found
quite enjoyable. But that
couldn't possibly be what was
making her so distant.

And that last moment we had
before Heather showed up? It felt
like someone had just plugged me
into an electrical socket. What
the hell was that about?

I mean, I'm not stupid, I know
what that was about for *me*. I'm
not a five-year-old. I know what
it feels like when two people
have that. . .

No. Bullshit. All this hobbling
is just screwing with my brain. We
didn't have that kind of moment. I
mean, maybe *I* did, but she was way
too busy hating my guts to be having that kind of moment.

Why am I even bothering to try
and figure her out now, anyway?
Heather just ditched me. She just

brought up a shitload of memories
that I'd much rather forget.

So maybe that's it. Maybe it's
just because I don't want to
think about Heather at all.

That merciless feeling was growing inside her again—the same feeling she'd had **chaos** the night before, the impulse to use more force than necessary.

I REMEMBER ALL YOUR SPEECHES

But I forgot all the words

Stuck to each other like hostless leeches

Don't you think our life was a bit absurd. . . .

That Prefight Fizz

CBGB was by far the best place to hear Fearless play: sweaty, dark, hot, and deafeningly loud. Every beat of the bass drum was a kick into Gaia's rib cage. This was exactly what she needed: Fearless pounding out brilliant songs to a massive crowd of freaks in a wild frenzy.

Brendan disappeared into the mob of dancers, but Paul and Gaia stuck together, stomping incessantly, feeding off every aggressive shoulder bump from the skate rats and twirling alterna-chicks. Why couldn't her daily life be more like this? Chaos without consequences. People who understood what was going on in her brain, as the lead singer and songwriter of Fearless always seemed to. And most important, no talking required. Paul and Gaia couldn't have heard each other if they tried. She signaled that she needed a bathroom break, and he made the universal sign for getting them something to drink by lifting an imaginary glass to his lips.

It took Gaia a moment to find her bearings, but she

managed to shove her way back from the stage and into the dark corridor that led to the bathrooms. She drew in a deep breath and caught the understanding smile of the last guy in the bathroom line—a smile that seemed to say, "Tough to breathe out there, isn't it?"

Her eyes narrowed.

That smile. In the shadowy red light it looked kind of familiar. . . .

Oh, shit. The smile belonged to Mick Butler: an asshole skinhead who used to hang around the park. Gaia hadn't seen him in months and hoped never to see him again. But no matter where she went, it seemed she was destined to run into the Village riffraff.

Mick lurched forward, revealing a friend in the shadows behind him. It was a fellow primate: a mountain of pale flab covered with pierces and tattoos.

"Hot damn, is that Gaia?" Mick shouted. He breathed the repellent stench of discount cigarettes and Jagermeister in her face. She did her best not to throw up in his. "Where the hell have *you* been?"

Gaia smiled humorlessly. "Avoiding you, Mick. Avoiding you."

"Ooh, same attitude." Mick laughed, putting out his cigarette on the floor and stepping closer. "But you look better. I could even say you look *hot.* You know what? I'd be totally willing to do you tonight. Is Mary here, too? My buddy could do her."

A vivid image suddenly flashed through Gaia's mind: that of her snapping Mick's neck and leaving him dead in a contorted heap on the floor. But she was trying not to go there tonight, to that dark place where she looked for combat. She was committed to having some nonviolent fun with the Moss brothers. This was family time. So she simply decided she'd wait to go to the bathroom. It wasn't an emergency. She could hold on for another few minutes. So she turned and pushed her way back into the crowd. Paul appeared seconds later from the bar area, holding two plastic cups.

"Here ya go," he said, thrusting one toward Gaia. "Ice-cold water. I figured that would be better than—" He broke off suddenly, his smile vanishing. His eyes locked on a spot just above Gaia's shoulder.

She whirled around. Mick and the primate were right behind her—only inches away. The stink of their sweat was almost overpowering.

Mick laughed. "Where'd you find this one? You been workin' that college boy circuit?"

Gaia felt a flicker of electricity in her veins: that prefight fizz. She shook her head, willing it away, then turned her back on him. "Ignore these two," she said to Paul. "They're not going to do anything here."

Much to her surprise, however, a coarse hand seized her arm from behind and spun her back around, knocking her drink to the floor. "No, I just told you, Gaia," Mick breathed into her face. "I'm going to do *you*."

Gaia sighed, very sadly. She didn't want to have to hurt him. She really didn't. Violence was her shadow, though. It followed her everywhere, even if—

"Get the hell off her!" Paul shouted, dropping his drink and throwing his body between them. But Mick's heinous friend snagged Paul by the wrist and twisted his arm behind his back, simultaneously flipping open an oversized blade with his free hand and holding it to Paul's face.

"Come on, Gaia," Mick moaned. "I need you tonight. Why don't you go find Mary and I'll do you both?"

The crowd around them immediately fell away, like a receding tide. That electric current was singing now, pumping through Gaia's blood. And it was accompanied by something else, too. Something relatively new. Yes. That merciless feeling was growing inside her again—the same feeling she'd had the night before, the impulse to use more force than necessary. But this time she didn't question it. Not when it came to this neo-Nazi waste of space who'd been stupid enough to let Mary's name fall from his mouth. . . or his partner, who'd made the very poor decision to draw a weapon on Mary's own brother.

Mick wriggled his eyebrows suggestively.

That was all she needed. In under a second she dropped into a state of total concentration, pinpointing the weakness of his grip. With a vicious jab she thrust her fist into his solar plexus, then hacked his arm away.

"Oof!" he gasped.

She caught a flash of his shocked, bulging eyes—then proceeded to whirl as he doubled over, lunging toward his repulsive friend. Clearly the friend had no idea how to respond to the attack because he simply gaped at her as she tore the knife from his fingers and freed Paul. Still spinning—and gaining momentum—she slashed down at Mick's crumpled body, slicing his arm.

"Jesus," Mick whispered. He collapsed to his knees. His hand immediately darted to the wound. Blood seeped through his fingers. He glanced over his shoulder. The fear in his wide eyes was plain. "You. . . you cut me."

But Gaia wasn't listening. She allowed the knife to slip from her grasp to the floor, well aware that the CBGB crowd was staring at her. Then she leaped into the air, spinning three hundred sixty degrees and simultaneously lashing out at Mick's partner's head with a roundhouse kick.

Her foot struck his flaccid cheek with a smack, and his neck snapped back. For a moment he stood at attention, his glazed eyes fixed on the ceiling. Then he simply pitched forward. He looked like a falling tree. Gaia smiled as he landed right on top of Mick, smothering him. She glanced at Paul.

Paul blinked at her. His face was white. He looked petrified.

"Are you okay?" she asked, panting. The music was beginning to fade.

He shook his head.

She opened her mouth but found she couldn't speak. The dark club danced and spun before her. She felt like she was looking through a curtain that was slowly being drawn shut.

"Look, I might faint, okay?" she managed to gasp. "Just get us a cab."

Paul's confused expression became fuzzy, and then everything went black.

TOM WAS BEGINNING TO WONDER about his own sanity, cooped up in that hotel room with nothing to do but reflect on the horrible nightmare and wait for a message from the informant. There was no clue as to when he might receive word. Each passing hour only served to feed the paranoia that sprang from his dream. Maybe he was just a sitting duck. Maybe there *was* no informant. The Agency could have been duped. It had happened before. This anxiously awaited communication might merely be a setup devised by Loki to get Tom out of the way.

But no. . . despite his fear, his instincts told him the informant was legitimate. It wasn't that he trusted the Agency. He simply knew how his brother operated. Loki was too proud and confident to resort to red herrings and decoys. He tended to take the direct approach, orchestrating events without concern for consequence and breaking human beings according to his will. He wouldn't see the need for precautionary tactics.

In fact, Tom's greater concern right now was the informant's life span. What were the actual odds that he could get to Tom before Loki got to him? If history could provide any indication, those odds were dismal—

There was a faint rustling at the door.

Reflexively Tom shot up from his seat at the desk and reached for the automatic pistol tucked into his jacket pocket. A small envelope slid under the narrow crack and onto the hotel-room floor. Keeping his pistol drawn, Tom jumped forward and snatched it up. He couldn't help but nod in satisfaction. Whoever this operative was, he was good. Few people could have evaded Loki for this long.

Tom tucked his gun away, then ripped open the envelope. Inside was a note and small silver key bearing the number 214.

Tomorrow 7:21 P.M.—the station Zoologischer Garten on the Hardenbergplatz. Track 8.
Box 214

Without a second glance, Tom placed the note in the hotel ashtray and dropped a lit match over it. He stared as the flames engulfed the paper and turned it to black ash. He could be back with Gaia in forty-eight hours, assuming all went well at the train station tomorrow. Assuming the informant could stay alive that long.

A Good Liar

SOMEBODY WAS SPEAKING ARABIC. Gaia could hear scraps of conversation, but she couldn't see a thing. Her eyelids fluttered, and she found herself staring up at a black surface, dancing with fast-moving light. She was lying on a soft, uneven cushion, and it was rumbling, bouncing.

Then suddenly a face appeared, looming just over hers.

"Are you all right?" Paul asked.

"I think so," she replied, clearing her throat. There was a crackle of static. It hit her: she was in a taxi.

"Do you want to sit up?" he asked. His skin was still pale, but Gaia couldn't tell if that was due to fear or due to the light of the passing streetlamps.

Gaia nodded, and with a couple of awkward shifts Paul helped her head off his lap until she was sitting upright. For a moment she stared at the back of the driver's head through the wall of bullet-proof glass that separated the front seat from the back. He was chattering on a CB radio in Arabic; he was asking someone about the best route uptown. . . . Gaia tuned out the harsh, guttural sounds. She glanced over her shoulder. Nobody was chasing them; there were no sirens, no shouts or rocks being thrown. They'd made a clean escape.

Paul seemed unsure what to say next.

"Uh. . . where's Brendan?" Gaia asked.

"He went back to his dorm." His voice was oddly flat and still. "I told him I'd take care of you. We're supposed to leave him a message that you're okay when we get home."

"I'm fine," she said. She frowned, shaking her head, trying to orient herself. The nondescript offices of Midtown flew by outside the windows. She must have been in the cab for at least ten minutes already. "What happened back there?"

He laughed shortly. "You don't remember?"

Gaia shrugged. "I remember cutting that guy Mick and letting the knife fall to the floor. Anybody else see that?"

Paul's smile vanished. He shifted in his seat. "Uh. . . if they did, they didn't do anything. They didn't say anything, either." He paused. "Anyway, I just kind of grabbed you and dragged you out onto the Bowery. Everybody got right out of my way."

"Thanks," Gaia muttered, feeling her cheeks flush. "I guess I—" She stopped in midsentence. Something the cabdriver was saying caught her attention. He was no longer asking for directions. No, now he was jabbering about something else—something involving a little girl's head in a boy's lap in the backseat and all the favors she was doing him.

She lurched toward the Plexiglas divider and smashed it with her fist.

"Be quiet!" she hollered in Arabic.

The driver fell silent, staring at her in the rearview mirror. Her eyes darted to Paul. He was staring at her, too.

"What language is that?" Paul asked.

"Arabic," Gaia mumbled.

Paul swallowed. "What was he saying?"

"Nothing," she replied. "He was being disgusting."

The driver clicked the CB again and resumed talking, this time in hushed tones. Paul didn't take his eyes off

Gaia. She kept her gaze fixed straight ahead, but she could feel the tension building inside him; she could feel his fear and puzzlement and awe swelling like helium in a balloon. She should have just kept her mouth shut. She should have never gotten into a fight at CBGB's. She should have grabbed Paul's hand and run when Mick and that moron had started trouble. She should have tried to be normal.

But then, she was never much of an actress. To be a good actress, a person had to be a good liar.

"Who *are* you?" Paul whispered.

Gaia turned toward the window. "You're asking the wrong person," she said.

Paul didn't say a word.

Central Park appeared on their left, a dark wilderness under a canopy of lifeless trees. Once again Gaia found herself zeroing in on the driver's speech. Had her Arabic gotten a little rusty? He was talking about her again; at least she was pretty sure he was—only she didn't quite understand the word he kept using to refer to her. It didn't sound like any of the derogatory terms that Arabs used for women. She didn't know *what* it was. Probably some new slang that was even more foul than anything she'd heard before.

A smile crossed Gaia's face. Here she was, worrying about the proficiency of her Arabic. As far as she went, that was about as close to "normal" as she could get.

She should be thankful.

SAM WAS BUZZING. THE ENERGY bordered on hyperactive. The night air was cold, but  he hardly noticed. His left leg wouldn't stop shaking as he leaned against the awning post of the Mosses' ornate Central Park West building. The doorman had been staring at him for some time, but he didn't care. He was still savoring the moment. He kept hearing that satisfying *crack*—the sound of his shoulder as it struck Josh's chin, smacking that goddamn smile off his face.

Why had he waited so long? He should have been pummeling Josh's face weeks ago instead of just dreaming about it. But the time had finally come. It was as if he'd snapped out of an endless daze. How long had he been sleepwalking? How many days running these ridiculous errands? How many weeks traipsing aimlessly around town like a paranoid zombie?

He'd actually walked all the way from NYU up to Central Park West. And he hoped "they" had watched him every step of the way. Because he didn't give a shit anymore. The time had come to strike back; the pieces were closing in, and if he didn't make a decisive move now, he was already checkmated.

The blow struck at Josh clinched it. He'd tell Gaia everything. They'd start from scratch. Tonight, not tomorrow. He'd just wait for her. As wired with emotion as he was, he'd wait as long as it took. All night would be fine. He certainly had no need to go back to the dorms. . . .

A cab pulled up to the building's entrance. Sam ducked down, trying to peer through the darkened window for signs of Gaia. *Yes!* His heartbeat picked up a notch. She was staring out the window with that faraway expression, the expression he'd never been able to interpret, no matter how hard he tried to dissect it—the expression he'd fallen in love with. The door opened, and she stepped out. He straightened and took a deep breath. Time to—

He stopped breathing.

Gaia wasn't alone. A guy followed her out of the cab and slammed the door behind them.

A *young* guy.

Sam shivered involuntarily. His gaze froze on this. . . kid.

This could not be what it appeared to be. Given all the torturous circumstances—given the moment of strained intimacy they'd shared only earlier today, there was simply no way. . . Sam couldn't even form the thought. His mind wouldn't allow it. Suddenly he wasn't cold anymore. He was very, very hot. His teeth ground together, and he sprang toward them on the sidewalk.

Gaia instantly jumped in front of the kid, as if to protect him.

Her eyes widened in baffled recognition.

"Sam?" she whispered. "What—"

"What the hell is going on here?" Sam demanded. He was aware of how silly and melodramatic that sounded, but the stock phrase came nonetheless: the stock phrase of the jilted.

Gaia frowned. "What do you mean?"

Sam's fiery stare shifted to the kid. "Who are you?" he spat.

"Paul," the kid answered shakily. He stepped out from behind Gaia.

"Paul," Sam repeated, stepping closer. He vaguely remembered that Brendan had a brother named Paul. But why was *he* out with Gaia? Gaia was friends with Mary, not—

"Paul, go ahead up, okay?" Gaia stepped between them again and ushered the kid toward the doorway. "I'll be up in a second."

Sam stood silently as Paul hurried under the awning, through the glass doors. He paused in the lobby beside the doorman. Both of them stared at Sam, but he was oblivious. His heart was pounding, fragmenting.

"What's going on?" he heard himself ask. "Why—"

A car horn blared. Sam whirled around.

The cab hadn't moved.

"Ignore him," Gaia mumbled. "He's an asshole."

Sam signaled for the cab to drive on. But there was no response. Suddenly the horn blared again. Sam flinched. The grating blast only fueled his rage. "Damn it!" he shouted. "Did you pay him or not?"

"Yes, we paid him." Gaia groaned. "Will you forget about it, please? If you have something to say to me, say it. I want to go upstairs. I'm tired."

"Tired?" Sam shouted, still glaring at the unmoving cab. "Well, what about me? I'm fighting for my goddamn life, and you're out with—"

Honk!

At that moment something inside Sam snapped. He marched over to the darkened window and pounded on it. Slowly the glass began to lower.

"Why the hell—"

Sam froze. There was a glint of metal in the shadows: the barrel of a gun, capped with a massive silencer.

It was pointed directly at Sam's chest.

"Ah salaam aleichem," a cold voice whispered.

A gloved finger squeezed the trigger three times. The shots were inaudible over the purring engine. Sam couldn't move. His legs went numb as he slapped his hands over his chest and watched the cab screech and take off down the street. Time had slowed down, almost as if it were doing Sam one last favor—allowing him to witness the moment before his death. Strangely, though, he felt no pain. He looked down to see the black holes . . .

But there was no blood.

There were no wounds.

No shots.

My God. The gun had been empty.

Sam's mouth fell open. Every part of his body shook. He scanned the street dizzily from left to right, tiny rivulets of sweat leaking down his temples. Central Park was suddenly a jungle war zone just across the street, with a potential gunman lurking behind every ominous rock, every misshapen tree, every crooked shadow.

"Sam?" Gaia asked.

Gaia. He had to get her inside. Now. He spun around and shoved her toward the door.

"Stop it!" she shouted, ducking away from his attempted push. "What's the matter with you? What did he say to you?"

"I . . ." He backed away from her. Then he realized what had happened: she hadn't seen the gun. Of course. He'd been standing right in front of the window. She wasn't supposed to see it. The blanks were just for him. And that was when he was struck by the full implications of what had really happened.

"That driver—he picked you up?" Sam croaked.

Gaia shook her head as if he were a stranger—or a lunatic. Her eyes were slits, her brow tightly furrowed. "You saw me get out of the cab, didn't you?"

Sam's eyes flashed back to the doorway, back to the doorman and the kid standing there, staring at him. They hadn't seen the gun, either.

"Get upstairs," he commanded.

"Sam, tell me what's going on—"

"*Now!*"

Gaia blinked. "You know, you should have warned me, Sam," she said.

"Warned you?" He jerked slightly. A wave of panic swept over him, blotting out even the terror. Did she know? Had she somehow figured out that he had put her life in jeopardy—

"You should have warned me you were such an asshole," she finished. She turned and marched through the doors.

Sam could only gape at her. On the other side of the glass the stares of the kid and the doorman were no longer frightened. They were threatening. The doorman was probably going to call the cops: "*Disheveled teenager lurking outside my building—send help.*"

Time to go. Sam shook off the subconscious wish that the cabdriver's gun had been loaded and sprinted down the sidewalk. It was strange: he'd experienced about a dozen of the worst possible emotions a human being could experience in less than sixty seconds. But in the wake of that onslaught, all he felt was clarity. He knew exactly what he had to do. He had to have another meeting with Josh. He had to go on the offensive. He had to eliminate the enemy. He would no longer be terrorized into submission. The chess game was just getting started.

She felt a pressing need to cast out the excess bullshit and remember what actually **talk** mattered **about** to **narcissism** her and, more important, *who* actually mattered to her.

"SO. . . UM, WHO WAS THAT GUY?" Paul asked, standing in his usual spot just on the other side of Mary's open doorway.

Gaia shook her head and flopped back against the pillows. "Good question," she mumbled. Yes, in fact, that was a *profound* question. Who was Sam Moon? Clearly he was many different personalities trapped in one body. There was Sam the liar. Sam the med student, who had once lived with Paul's brother. Sam the chess player. And now, it seemed, there was Sam the jealous ex-boyfriend.

This last identity was the one she couldn't quite figure out. But maybe that was the lesson to be learned from all this absurd drama and inexplicable behavior. Maybe even after all this time, she still didn't know Sam Moon at all.

No, no. Wrong thought. Pummel that thought until it bleeds. In fact, she didn't care much for any of the thoughts she was having. Every one of them needed to be knocked on its ass. The problem then became, however, that she was sitting in this room, and it was so quiet, and she was surrounded on all sides by Mary but without Mary—

"So?" Paul prompted.

"He's just. . . a guy I know," Gaia answered. It was a good thing Paul had never met him before; she didn't want to get into the whole Brendan-Sam connection right now. "Or don't know, depending on how you look at it."

Paul laughed. "Yeah. I think I understand."

Gaia sat up in bed and mustered a smile.

But Paul wasn't looking at her. He was staring down at his feet, his shaggy hair hanging in his eyes. He looked very young at that moment and very lost. Gaia had a flash of some feeling that she'd never felt before: she wanted to jump up and hug him—or to transform him magically into an egg and herself into a bird and keep him warm and safe in a nest hidden deep in a forest, far away from this room.

Suddenly he glanced up at her. "Where did you learn to fight like that?" he asked.

She bit her lip. "My father taught me," she said.

He nodded. "Oh. Well." His voice was distant and strained. He turned abruptly. "I. . . uh, think I better go to bed. Good night." He shuffled across the hall, then closed his door behind him.

Gaia chewed her lip. He probably thought she was a freak. He would be right, of course. She had to go to sleep. That was all she could do. She had to lie back again and think of absolutely nothing at all. Yes. It was an existential exercise, and she was good at that. She could simply wish herself into a deep abyss of nothingness. So she closed her eyes and sat there for a minute, letting the thoughts flow from her mind like dirty   bathwater   down   a   drain.

But in the silence her ears perked up.

She frowned. There was a muffled, sniffling sound coming from the hall—

Paul is crying.

Gaia held her breath.

Mary's brother was in his room alone, not ten feet away from her, in tears. Mary's brother was in pain. It occurred to her that on all those nights when Mrs. Moss had heard that sound behind that door, she might never have actually *opened* the door. She might have been afraid to intrude on his private moment. She might have been afraid that she wouldn't know what to say to him. Thankfully, being afraid was not one of Gaia's problems. She could march in there right now. They'd made a pact, after all. But would *she* know what to say to him?

It didn't matter. She'd figure something out. It had been quite some time since being fearless had served a nonviolent purpose. She jumped off the bed and marched into the hall, then knocked on Paul's door.

The crying ceased.

"Come in," he mumbled.

Gaia pushed open the door and found Paul sitting up against the head of his wrought-iron bed with his arms on his knees. He glanced up, making no attempt to wipe the tears from his face.

"Hey," she whispered.

"Hey. I do this sometimes. Don't be alarmed."

"I think I can handle it," Gaia joked softly. She hesitated, then sat down at the base of the bed. "Well, you screwed up, Paul. You're not following the rules."

Paul arched his right eyebrow. "What are you talking about?"

"You're sitting alone in your room, crying. Did you forget about our deal already?"

He smiled from the corner of his mouth and finally wiped the tears from his face with a swipe of his forearm. "Yeah, I guess I did. Sorry."

"It's all right," she said. "I didn't do any better." Gaia focused more intently on Paul's deep blue eyes, now tinged with red. "Are you okay?"

"Yeah." Paul looked down at his hands. "I miss her. I don't think it goes much deeper than that."

Gaia nodded. She knew exactly what he meant. She couldn't remember hearing anything that she would term as inspirational since her mother was alive, but something about the simplicity of Paul's statement had managed to inspire her. That ability not to over-complicate matters—it was a skill Gaia was sorely lacking. She'd spent so many hours running and rerunning situations in her head, and it only led to more confusion. Ed wasn't Ed. Sam wasn't Sam. Her father had disappeared again. But maybe she just missed them. All of them. The way they used to be. Maybe it didn't go much deeper than that. Maybe. In any event, Gaia felt the tightness in her chest beginning to evaporate. She shifted position, relaxing against the bars at the base of the bed.

"So," she said, looking at Paul across the distance of his mattress. "You know the rules. Now we have to do something completely random. Something totally unexpected."

"Right," Paul concurred, leaning slightly toward Gaia. He locked eyes with her as the room fell quiet. "But can we do it tomorrow? I'm exhausted. You know, it's, um. . . it's been a while since my last knife fight."

Gaia smiled. "Sure. But what are we going to do tomorrow?"

"Well. . . I'm playing football with some guys in the park. We do it every week down the hill from the carousel. Do you want to go? That's *reasonably* random."

"Football, hmmm?" She tapped a nail against her chin and thought about this for a minute. Two words jumped to mind: *safe violence.* Her smile widened. "Definitely."

Paul grinned. "Ten-thirty tomorrow morning, then. It's a date—or not a *date,* but. . . an agreed-upon time of gathering—"

"Right," Gaia interrupted, feeling an odd tingle of energy. "I'll be ready."

"Okay." Paul's grin relaxed into a peaceful smile. "Good night."

"Good night," she said.

She slid off Paul's bed and left his room, feeling surprisingly content. This brother thing definitely had its advantages. When she stepped back into her room, she actually found she was on a mission. Paul had inspired her to *un*complicate things. He'd given her a sudden burst of motivation. She felt a pressing need to cast out the excess bullshit and remember what actually mattered to her and, more important, who actually mattered to her. And one person in particular had been troubling her all day. She flipped on Mary's computer and logged on to her e-mail to set things straight.

From: gaia13@alloymail.com
To: shred@alloymail.com
Time: 11:41 P.M.
Re: Just ignore me

Ed,
    I want to apologize for this morning. I don't really know what happened. You were the only reason I even bothered coming to school. I guess the trouble started when I came to see my friend Ed, and instead I saw this tall guy who

<DELETE>

Ed,
    I don't know how to say this, but I saw you

today, and I missed seeing you in a wheelchair

<DELETE>

Ed,
    Sorry about this morning. It seems I'm just
not very comfortable with a walking Ed Fargo

<DELETE>

Gaia smacked her hand down on the desk.

This wasn't working. She hated every word she was putting on the page. How selfish could she be? *Ed, I'd prefer if you didn't have a miraculous recovery because it's making me uncomfortable.* Talk about narcissism. That was just plain sick. Besides, what was making her so uncomfortable, anyway? It wasn't like the lack of a wheelchair made him a complete stranger. What if he'd grown a beard? Would he still be Ed with a beard? Of course he would. What the hell was her problem? And here she was overcomplicating again. She had to keep it simple. She had to say what was important and nothing else.

From: gaia13@alloymail.com
To: shred@alloymail.com

Time: 11:41 P.M.
Re: Just ignore me

Ed,

   I'm sorry about this morning. I can't
explain what I felt, other than that I was suddenly looking at a stranger

<DELETE>

She flipped off the computer and stepped away, squirming with discomfort. She couldn't write a satisfactory e-mail. She was obviously incapable of keeping her apology simple. There probably was a reason for that, though—and it annoyed her. She couldn't keep it simple because the trouble between her and Ed was complicated.

ED JABBED HIS BEDROOM DOOR OPEN with the base of his right crutch, adding one more black smudge to the postmodern collage that now covered the bottom of the door. He'd actually mastered the routine of getting into his room by himself. There was a four-

Annoying Irony

step process. Step 2: Poke the door closed with left crutch. Step 3: Throw both crutches onto bed, simultaneously falling down into desk chair. Step 4: Writhe in agony as pain shoots up spine for next five minutes.

Welcome back to the world of bipeds, Fargo!

And so it went. Ed gritted his teeth, his eyes tightly closed (as they always were during step 4), wondering what his testosterone-addled physical therapist, Brian, would have to say about this latest accomplishment. Probably something along the lines of: *"You* rock, *baby! You da man! You da man! You're doin' it for Kid Rock and Freddy Durst and all the playaz!"*

Ed shook his head. He managed a miserable laugh between tortured gasps, and gradually the pain in his back began to recede. At least the pain took his mind off Heather. He slumped back against the seat cushion and opened his eyes. His room was cold and still, offering no comfort. The harsh overhead light bore down on him. Now, in the wake of the pain, came another sensation he'd been dreading far more. The sensation of guilt.

He didn't get it. Everything that she'd said made Ed feel like the biggest bastard on planet Earth, and most of it wasn't true. Or at least half of it wasn't true. The part about blaming her for the accident sure as hell was about as far from truth as a person could get. Honestly, at this point he really had no idea what was true and what wasn't. Or maybe he was lying to himself about that . . .

Gaia could help him. Gaia could talk him through this. She could tell him that he was an idiot, and Heather was a self-absorbed bitch, and could he please not call her anymore so late? He tried to smile again at his own lame joke, but he couldn't. Fantasizing about a conversation about Gaia only added to his guilt.

But that didn't make any sense. Why *shouldn't* he want to talk to Gaia? She was his best friend. He glanced at his computer, at his tired and distorted reflection in the blank screen. Right. She *was* his best friend. He jabbed his finger at the power button, then logged on to his e-mail and began to write.

From: shred@alloymail.com
To: gaia13@alloymail.com
Time: 12:06 A.M.
Re: Just a suggestion . . .

G$—
    Could we maybe just pretend you didn't turn evil this morning? Because right now, I am what is commonly referred to as "a friend in need." We don't even need to talk about that strange

<DELETE>

G$—

    I know it must be a little weird to see me
on my feet. Was that the problem this morning?
That was why you were acting so weird, right?
Because I felt this

<DELETE>

Gaia,

    Heather thinks that I am in love with you.
And I think she's

<DELETE>

    Ed shoved his chair away from the computer. If
Gaia read one of those e-mails, she'd never talk to him
again. Of course, that might solve some of his problems: it would make his life a hell of a lot less complicated. He stared at the monitor for some indefinite
period of time—a minute or five; he wasn't really sure.
He had no idea what to do next, either. Finally he blew
out a long sigh of resignation, pulled his chair back to
the desk, and typed something more appropriate.

From: shred@alloymail.com
To: heatherg@alloymail.com
Time: 12:21 A.M.

Re: Tomorrow

Heather,

Tonight was awful. Let's never have another night like tonight. You said what you had to say; now I just wanted to say three things:

1. I've never blamed you for my accident.
2. I am not in love with Gaia Moore.
3. I love you.

Do something with me tomorrow, okay? Or, I guess now it's today. Let's hang out.

It doesn't have to be this bad, Heather. It certainly couldn't be any worse than tonight.

Love,

Ed

From: heatherg@alloymail.com
To: shred@alloymail.com
Time: 12:45 A.M.
Re: Tomorrow

I think maybe you're right. I went home feeling horrible. I don't ever want another night like tonight either, Ed.

Maybe we can sort of start from scratch.

I'm going to a Hamptons reunion brunch at Sarabeth's tomorrow (I mean today). Put on something nice and meet me.

And don't worry, Chad Carmel will *not* be there, and neither will any of those people. Trust me, I've checked with Carrie about fifteen times.

Pick me up at 12:30. I promise to be nice if you will.

Do you own a pair of khakis?

Love,

Heather

Ed blinked at the screen. He wasn't sure quite what he felt. All he knew was that the feeling was very unpleasant. But he kept returning to one thought. The annoying irony of his situation had not escaped him. Not at all.

Regaining the use of his legs had left him completely paralyzed.

THE MOMENT JOSH OPENED HIS dorm-room door—with that twisted smile pasted on his chiseled face—was one of the happiest Sam had enjoyed in days. Because in that moment Sam was finally able to live out a long-standing

White Light, Red Light

dream: to remove the smile with his fist.

Josh never even saw the punch coming. His eyes were heavily lidded. It was late, and he was obviously tired, so he wasn't quite as guarded as he should have been. And as Sam's arm flew toward Josh's chin in the expanded silence, Sam soaked in every aspect of his tormentor's disguise. The droopy boxers. The ratty T-shirt. The mussed hair. *I was so perfect, so ingenious.* Josh Kendall *was* a college student. There was no way anybody would be able to mistake him for anything else. And within a matter of seconds he'd be a dead—

Thwack!

Josh's legs crumpled the instant of impact.

"Ow!" Sam howled.

The punch had *hurt.* He shook his hand as Josh fell to the floor. His pinky throbbed in acute pain. He stared at it, eyes wide, breath coming fast, wondering if he'd broken his finger on Josh's chin. It didn't seem to be crooked, but he could barely move it. His heart began to race. Josh was already recovering, already stumbling up on all fours and lunging toward Sam's legs. Sam tried to sidestep him, but he was too distracted. Josh's shoulders slammed into his shins, and Sam went toppling over him into the room.

"You idiot," Josh grunted.

Sam's face skidded across the rugged, industrial dormitory carpet. It was like sandpaper, burning his skin. He tried to roll away from Josh, to get his bearings, to strike again. But at that moment something struck the small of his back. Quite simply, it was the sharpest, single most excruciating pain Sam had ever felt. White light exploded in front of his eyes. He didn't even know what had caused it—an elbow, a fist, a knee. It didn't matter. His body went limp.

The fight was over.

The next thing Sam knew, Josh had twisted his arm behind his back, and Josh's free hand was at his neck, firmly squeezing and nearly cutting off his circulation. Sam couldn't move. He could hardly breathe. He tried in vain to struggle, but he was too weak. That blow to the back had somehow sapped all his energy. It was as if a plug had been pulled.

"Stop it," Josh commanded. "Don't be an idiot, Sam. Didn't I tell you not to get cocky? Wasn't I trying to help you out? Now look what you did." He twisted harder until Sam's entire arm had gone numb from pain. "Look!"

All at once a blinding red light flashed through Josh's dorm window, assaulting Sam's eyes. He blinked, fighting to turn away, but the viselike grip around his neck prevented him from moving.

"Do you see that light, Sam?" Josh whispered.

Sam nodded. The light suddenly dropped down to his chest. It was a glowing red dot, no bigger than a dime, very jumpy and shaky. Sam stared at it as it settled in the area of his heart.

Josh's lips were at his ear. "Do you know what that is?" he breathed.

"Yes," Sam said quietly. He swallowed. He'd seen enough movies to know a laser gun sight when he saw it. His muscles relaxed involuntarily. For a moment he was worried he might actually lose control of his bladder. The light disappeared, and Josh yanked him back from the window—hard.

"Now are you going to chill?" Josh's tone was sickeningly sweet.

"Yes," Sam conceded through clenched teeth.

Josh let go. Sam staggered away from him, rubbing his throbbing arm and neck. He tried vainly to ignore the dull ache in his back. His energy wouldn't return. He wanted to bolt from the room, but he couldn't seem to catch his breath. Josh sighed, then stepped over to the mirror. A red welt was beginning to spread from the gash on his jaw. He chuckled softly.

"That's a decent punch, Sammy. I'm impressed."

Sam just looked at him. He had visions of bashing his head against the dresser. Unfortunately, that would get him shot. He shoved his rage into a corner of his mind. He had one option left: the direct approach.

"Josh," he said. He tried to sound as neutral as possible. He didn't want to sound pleading or whiny or desperate. Just matter-of-fact. "I have to end this thing. Please. I'll do whatever they need me to do. Just let me do it now."

There was a half minute of silence as Josh continued to stare at himself in the mirror. Finally he turned away and shrugged, almost apologetically.

"I told you we're almost there, Sammy." He sat on his unmade bed. "So I don't know what you're throwing punches for. That's poor judgment. For a chess player, I would think—"

"Someone almost killed me!" Sam heard himself shout. His voice was hoarse. "What did I do? I've done every one of your goddamn deliveries, and someone fires a gun at me? He could have killed Gaia!"

"Shh-sh-sh." Josh frowned at him and brought his finger to his lips. "Chill, remember?"

Sam looked down at the floor.

"But did he?" Josh asked lightly.

"Did he what?"

"Did he kill you?"

"No, but—"

"Well, there you go, Sammy." Josh reached for a tissue on his nightstand and wiped the blood from his face. "Sounds to me like they were just making a point. You must have done something to piss them off. What were you doing at the time?"

"I . . ." Sam dropped down into the chair next to the bed, utterly deflated. He felt so beaten that he wasn't even bothered by Josh's "innocent curiosity" bullshit. Josh knew exactly what Sam had been doing at the time. Sam had been trying to see Gaia. He'd been breaking the rules. And now he was paying for it. What had made him think for a moment that he could take any control of his situation? They were everywhere. They were pointing guns with laser sights from buildings he couldn't even see.

"I was trying to talk to Gaia," he confessed, as if it were even necessary.

"Yeah, I figured," Josh murmured. His phony sympathetic voice was almost as offensive as his smile. "Listen, as your friend, I gotta tell you, Sam. . . I don't think you two are meant to be together. You know what I'm saying?"

Sam looked at him. That was the first time Josh hadn't called him "Sammy" in days. He was clever, Josh—more clever than Sam had even realized. Here he was, talking to Sam like a genuine friend. . . and for an instant Sam almost believed him. Sam was *that* much of a wreck. Either that or Josh was that skilled of a torturer. Or maybe both.

"Things just sound pretty rocky to me," Josh continued in the silence. He stood and stepped toward Sam, giving him a hard pat on the back. "I've been there, dude, and I'm telling you. . . I think it's time for you to move on. It might just be the ticket to ending this whole—"

"Go to hell." Sam swatted Josh's arm off his back, knocked over his chair, and marched for the door. "We're through talking."

"I'm just trying to help you, Sam. I've got a little more information than you, that's all. I mean, how well do you really *know* Gaia?"

In spite of every ounce of better judgment, Sam stopped at the doorway and turned. "What do you mean?"

Josh sat back in his bed and made himself comfortable. "Well, you probably don't need to hear this right now. But like I said, it's for your own—"

"*What?*"

"Well. . . what's the best way to put this?" Josh clasped his hands over his chest and gazed thoughtfully at the ceiling, looking for just the right words. "Let's just say that Gaia and her new friend were getting *pretty* cozy in the backseat of that cab."

Sam shook his head, almost awestruck by Josh's capacity for the depraved. "You're a liar," he murmured.

Josh smiled. But with the swelling under his mouth, the expression looked more like a sneer or grimace. At the very least, that brought Sam a fleeting moment of satisfaction. He'd done *some* damage. At least the smile was closer to what it truly represented.

"I'm just trying to warn you," Josh said.

"You're a bastard," Sam said shakily. He turned and

strode back to his own room. But once he'd closed his door behind him, fear began to chip away at him. He'd never admit this to Josh's face, but in the privacy of his room he could at least admit it to himself. He'd called Josh a liar. But the sickening truth was that he had no idea whether Josh was lying or not.

Memo

To: L
From: J
Date: February 27
File: 776250
Subject: Messenger

Scare tactics effective. Messenger has been disciplined. Liberation of subject is imminent. Awaiting further instructions.

Memo

To: J
From: L
Date: February 27
File: 776250
Subject: Messenger

Monitor messenger closely. Contact QRs. Neutralization of the leak is our priority.

Chad

Carmel. All you have to do is hear the name and you know he's a blond-haired asshole on skis. Chad's the kind of guy who wears thick white turtleneck sweaters and mirrored sunglasses. Who runs his hands through his hair every twenty to thirty seconds to make sure the swoop is just right. Who will tell you where to get the best cigars even though he's sixteen years old. You know the kind.

But maybe he's changed. How the hell should I know? I've changed, after all. The last time I saw him was a few years ago. He must be in college now, one of those third-rate but somehow respectable schools where the admissions process is based entirely on your family's tax bracket.

It wasn't until Heather mentioned his name in her e-mail that I realized I've hardly thought about my accident in at least a year. I mean, I've thought about the effects of the accident every

day, but not the accident itself.
I don't replay it over and over in
my head anymore. I don't dream
about it every night like I did
for the first year.

I used to pinpoint the moment
when I lost control. I'd dissect
that split second so it stretched
into a minute, an hour, a week. I'd
make the adjustment in my imagina-
tion so that I'd avoid losing control altogether—just do a quick
roll and then jump right back up
off the ground, still on my feet
with only a few minor cuts and
bruises. I haven't done that in so
long. I haven't really done it
since around the time I met Gaia.

But I think that being back on my
feet has made me think about it
again. That and hearing Chad's name.

We were staying at Chad's house
in the Hamptons when it happened.
The accident, I mean. It was
Heather and me, and Carrie Longman,
and then a bunch of Heather's "East
Hampton friends" as she called
them. I would have just called them

her "spoiled stuck-up rich asshole friends." I think that describes them more clearly than Heather's term. It was a little strange being in love with a girl who could have friends like that, but what can I say? They aren't much different than Tina and Megan and the other "FOHs," as Gaia likes to call them. They were just a few more friends to ignore.

Looking back on it now, though, once I'd spent ten minutes with those people, I should have told Heather we were going right back home. But Heather really wanted them to like me, and I guess I didn't want to let her down. I mean, she was so freaked about me meeting her "East Hampton friends," she actually forced me into the Gap and bought me some new clothes. Mostly I remember the *khakis*. I tried on so many goddamn pairs of *khakis* that day, I thought I'd turn that sickly shade of beige myself.

It was kind of comical, though, because usually she appreciated my

whole baggy-pants, skate-rat vibe.
This time she just wanted to sweep
it under the rug. She wanted me to
be someone I wasn't. I should have
known then that the weekend was a
bad idea. I guess I was young.
(Read: stupid.) And in love.
(Read: clueless.)

Anyway, the weekend was a nightmare from the get-go. Her friends
kept staring at me like I was part
of a different, undiscovered
species: *Homo skate-ien* versus *Homo
trust funderous*. I'm also not sure
if they'd ever seen a "poor" person
before—poor meaning somebody with
less than eight figures in the
bank. Especially Chad Carmel, whose
house looked like one of those com-
pounds from *The Godfather*. I'd
never really encountered anyone
like Chad before. I'd been under
the impression that guys so one-
dimensional and nauseating really
only existed on bad TV pilots—the
teen shows that don't even make it
to prime time past the first
episode. I was very wrong.

But I digress.

So I can't even remember how it came to this (my doctor blames this memory loss on something called repression), but for some reason, toward the end of that first Friday, Heather became obsessed with this dare. She was daring me to skate this incredibly steep winding hill that Chad had pointed out—Cannon's Hill or Dannon's Hill or something. She wouldn't leave it alone.

Now, obviously the irony of this whole scenario was that at first, she'd wanted me to fit in. She'd wanted me to be like Chad. Just for the weekend, I assume. Or at least I pray. But when she saw how her friends were ignoring me or just treating me like the help—*"Oh, hey, Ed, would you mind getting us another round of diet sodas?"* (Chad actually asked me this, in his own freaking house)—she decided to take the opposite approach. She decided that she wanted me to be an ultrabadass.

She wanted me to be *über*-Shred.
She wanted me to impress them
because clearly I wasn't very
impressive.

Anyway, she kept going on about
how *Chad* didn't think I could
skate this hill. She was turning
it into a big public thing in
front of her friends, playing up
the dare for the crowd. She probably figured good old Shred would
win them over with my I'll-try-
anything-twice attitude and my
skills on the board.

I didn't end up having much of
a choice. It was humiliating
enough wearing the khakis. I
wasn't about to add to my public
humiliation by backing off of a
dare from my girlfriend.
Especially if *Chad* didn't think I
could do it. You may think that
you could have said no in that
situation, but you're lying to
yourself. Believe me, with Chad
standing right there and your own
girlfriend daring you to your
face, you'd do it. You'd know

that it was an extraordinarily
moronic thing to do and that
you'd probably get yourself
killed. And you'd do it, anyway.

And that's what I did.

I didn't do it for Heather,
even. Not really. I did it for
myself. Because I bought into her
whole stupid mind game. I wanted to
show those assholes that I *was*
über-Shred. I took that hill so
fast that they had to follow me in
Chad's car. It was exactly what
you'd expect—the boys trying to
mess with my head and the girls
cheering me on as I ripped through
the sharp turns. I crouched so low
that I had to hold on to my board.
The trees on the side of the road
were whipping by me. If there was a
protruding branch, I'd duck. If
there was a pile of rocks, I'd jump
it. And I must say, it was by far
some of my finest work. I really
had no way of knowing that one of
the wheels on my board was faulty.

I would have made it fine with
all four wheels, but when you

lose a wheel going forty to fifty miles an hour down a hill, surrounded by trees, one of two things will happen. Most likely you'll die. Or else you'll end up like I did. I was lucky. As lucky as a kid who gets catapulted directly into a tree at that speed could be. The skateboard company insists that you'll never lose a wheel. Hence the settlement. Hence the $26-million liability.

I can't say I remember much after that. Not until the hospital. That's the first time I saw that look on Heather's face. It's the same look she's had anytime the accident has come up, which we do our best to make sure doesn't happen. It's an emotion that I think goes beyond guilt. I don't think it has a name.

So when she brought it up on the street last night, I was shocked. But I suppose it makes sense. With all this talk about my recovery and my settlement, I guess we've both

had the accident on our minds more.
And I still can't figure out why
she tortured herself so much over
it. I know she did, not that she
would ever admit it. I guess she
realized that she'd been pushy. She
would not take no for an answer
even when I, the most insane person
I knew at the time—even Shred
Fargo—thought it was too dangerous.
I don't think I've ever seen her be
that insistent about something
since.

   No, actually that's not true.
I have seen it since. When she
started asking me to lie about my
recovery. That's the same
Heather. That's the Heather that
got me to go down that hill. But
I don't blame her for the accident. I mean, if any of those
other girls had dared me, I probably would have blamed them.

   But not Heather.

He was buck
naked. Water
dripped from
his **danger**
lithe body
onto the
enamel tile.

ORIENTATION WAS STILL A PROBLEM. Once again Gaia woke up and had no idea where she was. Her immediate instinct was to smother her face with a pillow and sleep through all the depressing sunshine streaming through the blinds, but the fresh smell of fabric softener sparked her memory. It was her first clue that she was no longer alone.

Tenuous Morning Buzz

The pillowcases at Mercer Street always reeked of the faint stale odor of an enclosed space that hadn't been cleaned in days. Everything there smelled that way. But here at Mary's house there were many scents, and each stirred a feeling of contentment: the light clean sheets, coffee being brewed, eggs being scrambled. It smelled like a home—at least, the way she imagined a home *should* smell. The truth was, she really had no idea.

Gaia took three deep relaxing breaths and then rolled off the bed with a faint smile. Time to get up. Time to be normal. This was her plan: she'd have a quick shower, put on some extremely comfortable clothes, sit around the breakfast table—and then it was off to Central Park to frolic with some handsome college boys in the fields and play some football. It was a day in somebody else's life. Whose life was it, though? One of the beautiful people? Heather Gannis? She almost laughed out loud.

Then she caught a glimpse of herself in the mirror of the bureau. The smile faded. So much for the tenuous morning buzz. Her eyes were ringed with dark circles, her skin pallid, her hair a tangled mess. Somehow the reflection was a stark reminder that the life she lived was her own and nobody else's. She was not one of the beautiful people, nor could she ever pretend to be. And she was still a stranger here, an outsider. A guest. No amount of hospitality could change that.

Don't think, she reminded herself.

She rubbed her eyes and stumbled groggily out into the hall toward the bathroom. Thinking led to self-absorption led to misery. She had to stop focusing on *herself.* She would focus on Paul, on the events of the day as they unfolded. She would observe and participate and experience, but she would not analyze. And that way she would—

"Hey! Whoa, there!"

Gaia froze.

Blood instantly shot to her face.

She'd thrown open the bathroom door without knocking. Paul was just stepping out of the shower. He was buck naked. Water dripped from his lithe body onto the enamel tile.

"Sorry!" Gaia whirled and slammed the bathroom door shut. Her eyes were wide. Her breath came fast.

Paul laughed. "It's all right. We're all born this way."

Gaia squeezed her eyes shut. The self-flagellation began. *You idiot. You moron. You fool. You shit head.* Why the hell hadn't she thought to knock? Actually, she knew the answer to that question. She hadn't thought to knock because knocking hadn't been an issue in a very long time. After all, when you lived in solitude, you were never in danger of barging in on anyone.

"Gaia?" Paul asked.

"Yes?" She groaned.

"Don't sweat it. It's the price of sharing a bathroom. It happened to Mary and me all the time. It comes with the brother-sister territory."

Gaia opened her mouth, then closed it. "Oh," she said finally.

Her embarrassment began to fade, and it was replaced with an emotion that felt oddly like. . . annoyance. But why? She was annoyed with herself, of course—with her own thoughtlessness and stupidity. But something about the simple directness of Paul's tone bothered her. And she couldn't figure it out. He was obviously thinking of her as a sister. And why wouldn't he? *She* thought of him as a brother. It made perfect sense. They were close. . . almost intimate. Even after such a short amount of time, he was comfortable enough around her to joke around about nudity. Which was perfect as well. Which was as it should be. So what was the problem?

There was no problem. Right. She had just been a little shocked. That was all. She was overthinking this.

The door flew open, and Paul strode by her, a towel firmly wrapped around his waist. He patted her shoulder with a wet palm.

"It's all yours," he said.

Gaia watched as he disappeared into his room.

Don't think, she reminded herself.

"OH MY GOD, YOU LOOK GREAT!" Heather gasped gleefully when Ed emerged from his apartment building. "Why don't you wear clothes like this more often?"

A Sucker for Sure

Ed paused outside the glass doors as they swung shut behind him. He should have known she would compliment him. And it pissed him off.

Maybe it had something to do with the fact that he'd never felt more uncomfortable in his entire life. It wasn't the crutches digging into his arms or even the khakis—which made his legs look like packages that had just been delivered by the U.S. Postal Service. It was this goddamn orange turtleneck sweater that his sister's fiancé, Blane, had given to him as a present.

That was the kind of guy Blane was. He thought it was the most generous act in the world to give a sweater to his future wife's poor, crippled brother. He kept on patting himself on the back about it. Never mind that the sweater itched like hell and practically cut off the circulation to Ed's head.

"Are you okay?" Heather asked, frowning at him in the harsh, late winter sunshine.

"Sure," Ed said.

Secretly he had been hoping that Heather would burst out laughing when she saw what he was wearing. This outfit was about as un-Shred-like as he could get. There was absolutely no question that he looked like a big hobbling orange Popsicle. A sucker for sure. In fact, this color combo was pretty much straight-up Chad Carmel. Blane and Chad had a lot in common, actually. They might even be the same person. Maybe there was a secret factory out in the Hamptons where they cloned rich, insensitive morons—then sent them out into the world to make it a more dismal place.

"What's wrong?" she asked, fighting to keep smiling.

"Nothing." Ed tried to smile, too. "You look beautiful." He wasn't lying. It was a warm day, warmer than it had been in months, so there was no need to bundle up. Heather was wearing an open black velvet jacket, a white T-shirt, a long black skirt. Her hair was down, rustling in the brisk wind. She was as close to perfection as any girl he'd met (at least on the outside). While Ed. . . well, Ed still had a ways to go.

Heather glanced down the sidewalk toward First Avenue. "Shall we?"

Ed lifted his shoulders. *Yes! There's nothing I'd rather do more than eat brunch at Sarabeth's with your snotty friends from the Hamptons!*

"I guess we should take a cab, huh?" Heather asked absently.

"Or we could just bag the whole thing," Ed mumbled under his breath.

Heather shot him a withering stare, then started down the street by herself. Ed rolled his eyes. That hadn't been a smart move. If he was going to get back on track with Heather, he had to keep his mouth shut. He hobbled forward and tried to catch up.

"Look, I'm sorry," he called after her. "It's just. . . I just can't stand your East Hampton friends. You know that."

She stopped and turned, scowling. "These aren't my *East* Hampton friends. I told you that Chad wasn't gonna be there, didn't I? These are my *South* Hampton friends. You actually think I'd make you see those people again?"

Ed stared at her. She wasn't joking around. She actually thought there was a difference between her East Hampton friends and South Hampton friends. He didn't know whether to be frightened or disgusted or appalled. . . or *what*. All he knew was that Heather Gannis didn't nearly look as stunning as she had only seconds earlier.

"We're going to be late," she stated coldly.

"Fine," he muttered.

She marched to the corner and quickly flagged down a cab, then delicately stepped in, making sure her skirt wouldn't wrinkle beneath her. The door stayed open. She crossed her arms and waited.

For a fleeting instant Ed considered turning around and limping home. But he knew that would be an act of finality, one from which there might be no return. So he doggedly struggled forward, handed Heather each crutch, then pulled himself into the cab. At the last instant, however, his foot caught on the doorjamb. He tumbled across the seat. Heather scooted out of his way, and he landed on the car floor. A sharp tingle shot up his spine.

"Ow!" he shouted.

"Come on," Heather grunted, yanking him into an upright position. "You're gonna be fine." She leaned across him and swung the door shut. "Sarabeth's, please," she called to the driver.

Ed grimaced at her, struggling to ease into the seat and ignore the pain at the same time. "You know, a little sympathy every now and then wouldn't—"

"Oh, shit!" She groaned.

"What?"

She eyed his legs, shaking her head. "Your *pants.* Now they're filthy." She glanced down at the car floor, wrinkling her nose in disgust. "It's dirty down there."

Ed's jaw tightened. "I fell," he said.

"I know, but look at your pants. I don't want to bring you in there with. . . *ugh,* forget it. I can't take you *anywhere.*"

He stared at her for another five long seconds. His blood was beginning to boil. There was no way she could possibly be—

"That was a *joke,*" she explained.

"High comedy," he mumbled.

They spent the remainder of the cab ride in silence.

The Great Machine

FRUSTRATION WAS BEGINNING TO set in.

Loki had obviously chosen the wrong team, and there was too little time to make changes. Now he was forced to participate in the one activity he despised above all others: waiting. Waiting for them to find Tom. Waiting for them to find the leak, the traitor who stood on the verge of betraying the intricacies of Loki's project. (The delicious beauty of the word *project* lay in its vast understatement.) Of course, he knew that in spite of all his planning—and a few minor successes and setbacks—all the years since Katia's death had ultimately been spent doing just that. Waiting.

He'd been waiting to reclaim what was his, to execute some long-required justice, to exorcize some of his sorrow. But most of all, he'd been waiting to accomplish something truly remarkable— something worthy of Gaia's respect and admiration, maybe even her love. And after all those years of extensive and enlightened patience, his various enterprises were paying off. The great machine had finally been energized, its many cogs starting to spin in unison across many time zones. Plans within plans were coming to fruition.

Yet here he was, sitting once again at his laptop in his sparsely furnished loft, with no other option but to wait some more. All he felt was a combination of barely restrained anger and impatience. He pounded out yet another instant message. Probably his hundredth in the last forty-eight hours.

Instant Message Board 20

L: Progress report

QR9: Enigma still out-of-pocket

QR10: No progress

QR11: No progress

L: Leak status?

QR9: No progress

QR10: No progress

QR11: Valid intelligence confirmed from Berlin. Following up immediately. May have a lock within thirty minutes.

L: Excellent. If leak is confirmed, we'll find Enigma there as well. Assigning QRs 1-4 to Berlin immediately. When leak is determined, terminate. Do not wait for orders. We cannot proceed until security has been reestablished.

Loki breathed a sigh of relief. He nodded in satisfaction. Finally some competence. It was about time. If they could confirm the identity, then the leak was as good as dead, and they could finally proceed—with Tom under surveillance again. Loki had no doubts that the leak would lead them directly to him. The final loose thread would be clipped.

He typed the necessary memo and sent it off through the secured server. Once he'd received his response, he rose from his seat and began to pace slowly toward the window and back again, assessing the remaining tasks at hand.

Waiting was so much easier when the reward was assured.

ED HAD THE DISTINCT FEELING that he was in hell. No, purgatory. Right. That was where they sent you before you went all the way down to the fiery pits with the demons and the pitchforks and ironic punishments. Purgatory was more familiar. Purgatory was a place  you knew and hated in life, where you were forced to await your punishment.

That was Sarabeth's. It actually *looked* like a house in the Hamptons.

The whole place had a lame, phony French country inn vibe, at least as far as Ed could tell. Just like Chad Carmel's house. Everything was either white or cream colored, except for the pale blue design on the wallpaper and the big floral arrangement in the shelves of the center column, which was made up of blue flowers inside this huge sort of wheat. . . *wreath*. Was there such a thing as a wheat wreath? Ed had no idea. All he knew was that there weren't any greasy fat men in white paper hats running around with greasy plates of greasy eggs. *That* was breakfast.

All of a sudden he felt nails digging into his arm, nearly puncturing the puffy orange sweater.

"You know, maybe this was a bad idea," Heather whispered at his side. "I think we should just go."

Ed turned to her. He couldn't believe it. She looked almost as miserable as he felt: flushed and anxious. Was this some sort of miraculous change of heart? Was the Heather he loved—the *real* Heather—bursting out of her self-imposed Hamptons bubble and fighting to break free?

"I want to leave now," she whispered, increasing the pressure on his arm. Her eyes darted over her shoulder, back toward the door.

"Um. . . sure," Ed mumbled. Then he laughed. "What's the problem? Did you just realize orange and khaki was a bad color combo?"

"I'll tell you later, just—"

"*Heather!*" somebody called out from the dining area. "Heather . . ."

That voice.

Ed's insides seemed to clench, although he couldn't quite place it. It *was* familiar, though—grating and smarmy. Ed stared at Heather as her face switched in an instant from wide-eyed anxiety to a big, fake smile.

"Hi!" she sang out.

In that instant it clicked: Ed knew who he would see when he turned around. He would see himself. Thanks to those goddamn mirrored sunglasses.

No guns or
knives. Not
much blood.
Just some
pummeling,
which **steamy**
seemed to **hiss**
clear her
mind
completely.

TOM SLID THE KEY INTO BOX 214 and turned the lock. Sitting in the center of the empty aluminum locker was a slim black cell phone with a small yellow Post-it attached. As quickly as he could, Tom pulled out the phone and scanned the vast, smoky hall of the train station for potential surveillance. His eyes sought out, then passed on a number of suspects: the overweight woman with her poodle, the nondescript businessman reading a newspaper. They were civilians, though. He knew it. They met his gaze. Agents were always the ones who wouldn't stare back at you.

So. It seemed as if Loki still hadn't located him. Which meant that there was still a minuscule chance that Loki hadn't gotten to the informant, either. Tom quickly hurried toward the rest rooms, examining the Post-it. His feet clattered on the stone, lost in the reverberating voices and loudspeaker announcements.

Frequency 74993. Wait for my signal.

He stuffed the note deep in his pocket and abruptly changed direction, heading briskly toward track 8. *Please let him make it this far,* Tom prayed. The station Zoologischer Garten was massive—inundated with equal numbers of Germans and tourists. The blaring sun was reflecting twice as brightly off the huge steel-and-glass train platform on the main concourse. Tom removed his sunglasses from the front pocket of his black overcoat and slipped them on, constantly checking for tails in every available reflective surface: the metal of a garbage can, a coffee cart, the window of a magazine shop.

Suddenly he spotted a German family, with a young daughter about the same age as the girl from his nightmare. . . the same age as Gaia when they had last been a true family. This girl was also blond. For a moment Tom's concentration wavered. He shook his head violently and picked up his pace—a stupid move, as it attracted attention to himself. But with Gaia's life quite possibly at stake, his long-honed professional armor was beginning to show signs of wear. The nightmare was still haunting him.

I'm with you, Gaia. I'm with you right now. I haven't abandoned you. Everything I do now is for you.

With a final surreptitious glance over his shoulder, he climbed the stairs to the platform. The sunlight warmed his face. Track 8 was relatively deserted. There were only one or two people on both sides of the track. The informant had made a good choice. If they survived this transaction, the informant deserved a medal and a pension from the agency. Tom would vouch for him.

Whoever you are, I owe you one, friend.

A man in a black cap and beige overcoat walked up

onto the opposite platform. For a moment he seemed to look across the tracks at Tom, but he didn't look directly at him. He paced a bit. Checked down the track for the train. Checked his watch. This was the man. Tom was certain of it.

A train appeared from around the bend, sounding its horn. As the horn grew louder and the train neared the station, the man in the beige coat suddenly pulled out a small black cell phone and began to dial. Tom felt a flicker of hope. He thrust his hand in his pocket and whipped out his own phone, pounding the frequency code into the keypad. Again the horn sounded, deafeningly. The platform vibrated. Tom slapped the phone against his ear, switching his gaze back and forth between the informant and the train. The informant was obviously planning to deliver his message and immediately board the train, but what about the noise factor and the potential interference? And the lack of time—

"Can you hear me?" a deep, emotionless voice asked through a sea of static.

"Just barely," Tom hissed. He glanced toward the train again. They had maybe fifteen seconds before the call was lost altogether.

"I'm sorry," the voice said. "This—*shhh*—best—*shh*—could do."

"You're breaking up," Tom shouted. "Can we change frequencies?"

"I'm ru—*shhh*—of time. You—*shhh*—listen closely."

Tom's gaze shot back to the informant. A man had appeared directly behind him: a man in an overcoat and suit. He was folding a newspaper and beginning to walk toward the informant. Panic shot through Tom's veins.

"Behind you!" Tom whispered. "Move away from—"

"Listen—*shh*—me."

"Can you hear me?" Tom breathed, his eyes pinned to the slow-moving man with the newspaper. "Goddamn it, listen! He's right—"

". . . *shhh*—talk, just listen!" he insisted. "It's Gaia. . . they're planning a kidnapping—*shh*—operation involves DNA—"

The train sliced through Tom's line of vision, roaring into the station and cutting him off from the informant. He stood in silence, with the phone to his ear, his mind spinning with the words he'd just heard. He wouldn't jump to conclusions. He couldn't. They didn't make any sense. He swallowed, staring at the train as it stopped with a loud hiss.

A German voice blared from a loudspeaker. But the voice on the phone was silent. Tom forced himself to breathe deeply and evenly, waiting as the train filled with passengers, waiting for it to pull away, waiting and waiting. . . .

Finally, with another steamy hiss, the wheels turned and it began to rumble out of the station.

Tom's jaw tightened when he saw the empty platform. The informant was gone—probably dead already. He didn't waste another moment. He thrust the phone in his pocket, raced down the platform steps, and disappeared into the crowd. There was no time to consider the puzzle pieces of information he'd heard. Gaia was alone. Tom would be on a plane home within an hour. If not sooner.

THE OPPOSING TEAM HAD ALREADY

Transparent Hustle

come to fear her. As well they should. Nobody could tackle her, and nobody wanted to stand in her way, either. Gaia was having a blast. She'd just scored her second touchdown. It was so easy. All of Paul's friends kept staring at her with looks of bewilderment and awe. The question of the day seemed to be: "Are you *sure* you've never played football before?"

She hadn't, of course. But if she'd known what she'd been missing, she would have started a long time ago. She felt so *alive*—with her clothes all muddied and her cheeks rosy and the crisp air tearing into her lungs. On TV, football looked so boring. A bunch of guys stand really still, and then they pile on top of each other. Then they wait while idiot commentators make moronic remarks. And then they do it again. But now she understood the true nature of the sport, the *strategy*. In some ways, football was like chess. The pawns protected the king, which was the quarterback. Every play was another move. . . .But the best part of all was that football was an institutionalized means with which to express as much aggression as possible. No guns or knives. Not much blood. Just some pummeling, which seemed to clear her mind completely. There was no past, no confusion, no suffering—just a lot of easygoing camaraderie, the kind of bonding that people her age must experience on a daily basis all across the country. Normalcy was a beautiful thing. She'd underestimated it for far too long.

Time for another kickoff. Gaia stepped into a huddle with four of Paul's friends. She wiped her brow with her forearm, smiling at all of them. They glanced at one another and smirked. It was unbelievable. She was actually having fun. Her absurd escapist behavior plan was working.

"Ready for another kick?" one of them asked.

She nodded. Her team had already relinquished all kicking honors to her, insisting that her whole I've-never-played routine was a transparent hustle. They clapped in unison and then lined up at one end of the field, facing down Paul and his team at the other end.

Gaia placed the ball on the kicking tee.

"Ready?" she shouted.

Paul's team nodded.

With a deep breath she sprang forward and kicked the ball as hard as she could. It sailed high into the air, and she sprinted downfield—almost managing to catch up with it. Her intention wasn't to show off, but what the hell? She smiled as Paul backpedaled and positioned himself for the catch. She was going to nail him. This was going to be good. That wasn't quite working out, but it was still a hell of a lot better than the reaction she'd get if she kicked the ball as far as she could. She wasn't even sure she wanted to know how far she could kick it.

The instant the ball landed in Paul's hands, she focused her eyes on him like a tiger preparing to pounce. A few of his teammates tried to block for him, but she sidestepped them easily, as if they weren't even moving, as f they were stationary mannequins. She actually felt competitive. It was glorious. Paul started left, then quickly bolted to the right. Poor guy. He didn't know about martial arts training. She'd been trained to spot and react to that kind of rudimentary fake out since she was a little girl.

The distance between them closed. She could see Paul glancing at her out of the corner of his eye. He tried to pick up his pace. They both laughed out loud. And then she launched herself off the ground, flying headfirst into Paul's midriff, securing both her arms around his waist, tackling him hard to the ground and rolling him over twice.

Paul winced.

Gaia smiled down at him, straddling him, covered in dirt. "Are you all right?" she asked.

"Remind me to suggest basketball next week," he said with a groan.

"Are you kidding?" She laughed, keeping Paul pinned to the ground. "I'm having too much fun. I think—"

"*Gaia!*"

The sound of her own name sliced through the air—in a voice she didn't recognize, a voice choked with rage. And when she turned, she saw why.

She'd never seen Sam Moon look so angry.

"WHEN I HEARD THERE WAS GONNA be a Hamptons reunion brunch, I couldn't resist,"

Fake Smiles

Chad said, grinning from behind those ridiculous sunglasses. "I took the jitney straight in last night."

Ed stared at him, wondering why the hell he didn't take those glasses off. It wasn't *sunny* inside the restaurant. But maybe he just wanted to avoid making eye contact. Which wasn't a bad idea, actually. Maybe Chad was smarter than he looked, sounded, acted, and generally presented himself.

Note to self, Ed thought, matching Chad's fake smile. *Kill Heather and dump body in East River.*

At least she was painfully anxious and nervous. That provided him with some consolation. Her face was so stiff that it looked like it had just been taken out of a freezer.

"So, anyhoo, we're sitting back there in a private booth," Chad said, jerking a thumb over his shoulder. "Carrie and Muffy and the whole crew. Why don't ya come join us?"

Carrie and Muffy. He was being serious. Ed glanced at Heather. She kept her eyes fixed to Chad. She wouldn't even acknowledge that Chad had just used the word *anyhoo*. Even *Blane* didn't use that word. In less than a minute Chad had already surpassed Ed's future brother-in-law in terms of sheer heinousness—a feat that Ed wouldn't have believed was possible.

Chad patted Ed's shoulder. "So, it's great to see you back on your feet, Ted," he said.

"My name's Ed, Brad," Ed replied. His lips were beginning to hurt. He'd never smiled so much for so long.

"Right," Chad said, slapping his head for dramatic

effect. "Ed, sorry. And, uh. . . it's Chad."

"Oh, *Chad!*" Ed laughed his best socialite laugh.

Chad's sunglasses roved over Ed's crutches. "You must be so totally happy that you can, like, walk. . . or almost. . . ."

Ed nodded. "I totally am, bro. I totally am."

"Yeah," Chad murmured, nodding thoughtfully. "Hey, man, I really like your sweater, by the way."

A tiny squeak escaped Ed's lips—the beginning of a laughing fit. Heather squeezed his arm again. Hard. Ed bit the side of his cheek. But Chad didn't notice Ed's derision, or at least he pretended not to notice. Instead he frowned at Ed's legs.

"But, um. . . what happened to your pants?"

"What do you mean?" Ed asked innocently.

"They're like. . . *filthy.*" Chad glanced around the restaurant. People were beginning to stare at them, probably because they were standing right in the middle of everything, blocking the paths of waiters, and generally making an embarrassing spectacle of themselves. Ed realized that he no longer felt like laughing. He felt like smashing Chad's sunglasses with his fist.

"I fell getting into a cab," Ed said.

Chad shook his head. "That's really sad, dude," he said.

Ed wondered if he could detect the daggers shooting from his eyes. "Is it? That's funny, I didn't think it was."

Nobody said a word. Chad stared at Ed, and Ed stared at Chad—and who knew what the hell Heather was doing?

"You know, I'm actually really glad I ran into you today," Chad announced. He suddenly sounded very serious. "Because I've kind of always wanted to tell you—"

"*Ugh!*"

Ed flinched. All at once Heather was groaning. She doubled over and clutched her stomach.

"What's wrong?" Ed asked with a scowl.

"My stomach," Heather moaned. "I just got this really sharp pain. . . ."

She was lying, of course. She was a terrible actress. But Ed was thankful. At least she was making an attempt to disrupt the horror that had already gone on for far too long. And once again, if Chad knew she was faking it, he pretended to be oblivious.

"What's wrong?" Chad asked. "Too much booze last night?"

Heather's face darkened, but she kept gripping her sides. "No. . . I don't know. . . . I feel really sick, though. Ed, could you come downstairs with me?"

Ed stared at her. He was half tempted to tell her that he wouldn't, just to see her squirm. But then he would be stuck with Chad. This morning was really shaping up to be one of the best he'd ever had. It probably ranked at number three: right behind the morning he woke up in the hospital after the accident and the morning he found out that Gaia Moore was in love with Sam Moon.

"Of course I will, dear," Ed said. "But you'll have to carry my crutches and let me lean on you for support. How does that sound?"

Heather looked up at him, her face white as a sheet. "It sounds fine, Ed," she said in a tight voice. "Just fine."

SAM DIDN'T QUITE TRUST HIS EYES. He knew that he was putting himself in terrible danger by coming here, by wandering all up and down the island of Manhattan, searching for Gaia. He knew that he was putting Gaia in danger, too. Only now. . . now he no longer felt guilty. His motives were selfish, but clearly they were well-founded. He had to hear directly from Gaia that Josh's story was nothing more than a manipulative lie.

One of Them

First he'd gone to Washington Square Park. Then to Gray's Papaya. Then to the Mosses' fancy Upper West Side apartment, where he'd been politely informed by the maid that Paul and "his friend" were playing football in Central Park.

"*His friend.*"

Clearly Josh hadn't been lying at all.

Gaia was on top of Paul. Their legs were entangled, and their faces were only inches apart. Smiling. Laughing. Playing football. Since when had Gaia switched from chess to *football?* How could she possibly be doing this? She was sobbing to him in her father's apartment just over a week ago. Her father had abandoned her again, she'd said. Sam had let her down again, she'd said. She'd cried to him about how they would never make it work—about how she was alone in the world, how she was doomed to always be alone.

And now here she was, barely a week later, going out to clubs at night and playing football in the morning. With her *buddy*. The brother of a guy who thought Sam was a murderer. Sam knew what this was. It was all one huge vindictive slap in his face. Gaia was trying to drive him crazy with completely absurd behavior, the way he had done with her. It was her twisted way of getting back at him for destroying their trust. And it was some very successful revenge, he had to admit.

"Gaia!" he shouted again.

She rolled her eyes and pushed herself off Paul, then strode toward him across the field. Sam was very conscious of the fact that nine fairly large, muscular guys were all staring at him. He tried to put them out of his mind.

"What are you doing here?" she asked, folding her arms across her chest.

"I had to see it for myself," he answered.

She raised her eyebrows. "See what?"

"I had to see you rolling around in the dirt with Paul." The words were strained. Again he felt like he was outside himself, watching a stranger, somebody who had no relation to Sam Moon. Gaia shook her head and turned to walk away, but Sam grabbed her by the arm.

"You can't keep doing that!" he shouted.

"I can do whatever I want," she hissed. She clamped her hand on Sam's and removed it, spinning away from him. Her eyes were slits.

Sam swallowed. The emptiness inside was beginning to consume him. He felt like a shadow, a shell. There was nothing left, nothing but bitterness and acrimony. "Do you want to tell me the truth about you and Paul?" he croaked.

"The *truth?*" Gaia scoffed. "When was the last time you told me the truth about where you were going or where you've been?"

Sam flinched. A valid point. But he was too angry to give it any credit.

He stepped closer to Gaia and tried to lower his voice. "Is there something happening between the two of you or not?" The question was all that was left to him. It comprised his entire existence.

Gaia blinked. Then she laughed—a humorless, disgusted laugh. "He's like my brother, Sam," she mumbled. But there was a hesitant tone in her voice.

"What was going on with the two of you in the back of that cab?" he heard himself ask.

"I passed out after a fight!" she shouted with exasperation. "You've seen it happen before. Paul was just letting me—" Gaia froze.

"What?" Sam spat. "Letting you what?"

"Why would you think we'd done something in the back of the cab?" she asked again, glaring at him suspiciously.

Sam could feel his life collapsing in on itself. He was racked with images of all the people who'd given him that same stare—Ella Niven, the police, Brendan, Josh. . . and now Gaia. He was caught in the undertow of accusations, struggling against the tide. But what was the point of fighting it? Drowning was inevitable. He looked into Gaia's eyes and saw every single thing he'd done wrong. And he was quite positive he hated himself—for every lie he'd told her, and every stupid errand he'd run, and every jealous word that had come out of his mouth. He was turning into a hideous combination of everyone he despised.

He was turning into one of *them*.

There was no denying it. The transformation had

been insidious. And in spite of all his best intentions—despite all his self-motivational monologues and a couple of useless punches—he really hadn't done a thing to stop it. *This is the time,* he realized suddenly. *This is the time to stop this. This is the time to tell her everything. Right now, before anything else can go wrong.*

"Listen to me. . . ," he began, with all the gentleness that had been missing. He stepped as close as she'd let him, his eyes roving over her very sad face.

And then he stopped.

Because there, on her upper-right temple, was a small, glowing red dot, no bigger than a dime.

Memo

To: J
From: L
Date: February 28
File: 776244
Subject: Gaia Moore

Subject has been liberated. The messenger is in hand. Prepared to proceed as ordered.

Memo

To: L
From: QR11
Date: February 27
File: N/A
Subject: N/A

Leak has been terminated. Transfer of information incomplete. Enigma is in pocket, currently boarding a flight for New York. Prepared to proceed as ordered.

Memo

To: ALL CONTACTS
From: L
Date: February 28
File: N/A
Subject: N/A

We are now back on schedule.

Plan will proceed as of 6:00 P.M. Greenwich
mean time.

He wanted the
conversation
to end.
Before he
lost it **final**
completely.
Before **warning**
he got them
both shot.

"YOU KNEW HE WAS GOING TO BE
here, didn't you?" Ed asked, trying his best to find a happy medium between yelling and whispering. Unfortunately, the smelly foyer outside the rest rooms wasn't the best place for a private argument. But it would have to do.

Moralistic
Smoke
Screen

"Of course not," she hissed, glancing up the stairs. She'd dropped the sick act the moment they disappeared from Chad's view. "Seeing him was the last thing I wanted. Why do you think I want to go home?"

Ed just looked at her. "Heather, can I ask you something?"

She nodded, still peering up toward the main floor.

"Why did you even come here?"

"To see my friends," she mumbled.

There was more to it, though, and Ed knew it. Heather kept hoping Ed could overcome this inane class struggle with her "other" friends. Now that he could walk, he'd taken a crucial step toward accept-ability. Yet somehow, with his crutches and stained pants and sense of humor, he was letting her down yet again. And *that* must have been why Chad was making her so nervous. Of course. It made perfect sense. Chad was exactly what he could never be.

Not without lots more money.

"I have an idea," Ed announced. "Why don't I just have *another* accident, and then maybe I can pick up another twenty-six million?"

Heather jerked toward him, her eyes blazing. "What the hell are you talking about?"

He shrugged—at least as much as he could with crutches digging into his armpits. "You tell me."

"Don't do this, Ed," she warned. "Not here."

"Do what?" Ed asked.

She didn't answer. She simply shook her head. So did Ed. Heather could say all she wanted about his loyalties and betrayals, and his hidden feelings for Gaia, and what a horrible egregious sin it was to break a promise, but that was all a bunch of peripheral bullshit—Heather's big moralistic smoke screen. Because as far as Ed could tell, Heather had asked him to lie about his recovery for one reason. And it was the same reason she'd gotten so angry at him, the same reason she was giving him the silent treatment today, the same reason she was running from Chad Carmel.

Money.

Plain and simple. Nothing complicated about it.

For whatever skewed reason, Heather believed that her place in the world was dependent on the number of dollars in her bank account. She didn't know who she was without money and everything that came with it—privilege, preference, admiration, power. . . garbage. Ed had always tried to ignore that part of her. But just as her looks had improved through the years, her shallow values seemed to have gotten worse. Or simply more transparent.

"So are we gonna leave or not?" she asked in the silence. Her voice was a certain combination of plaintive and demanding that only Heather could have managed. "We can pretend I have food poisoning or something."

"If it's so unbearable for you, why don't you just go?" Ed suggested. "I'm hungry. I think I'll sit down with Chad and the rest of the—"

"Shut up," she snapped.

Ed straightened up on his crutches and looked her in the eye. "Fine. Just tell me why we're leaving, and I'll take you home."

Heather let out a loud frustrated groan. "It's not why you think, okay? It's not about rich or poor, or money, or how materialistic I am, okay? So can we just *go* now? Please. I'm sorry we even came. I thought I could prove something to you about how I've changed, but it was just a bad idea."

"Is it because there are people up there from that weekend?" Ed pushed.

Her face fell. "I don't want to talk about that weekend," she breathed. "I just want to go home, okay?" Her voice cracked. Her expression was as desperate as Ed had ever seen it. Those anxious, reddening eyes set against that white, quivering face. . . she almost looked like a mouse—one that was trapped in some cruel science experiment, overly traumatized and dying to escape.

A wave of shame enveloped him. He didn't want to be hurtful. He just wanted Heather to take a good look at herself. And clearly this was not the place for her to do so.

"Fine," he conceded. "I just need to use the bathroom really quick. Then I'll take you home and . . ." He found he couldn't complete the thought. Because he was worried about what would come out. The words on the tip of his tongue were *say good-bye*. And if he said that, he knew he would mean it for good.

Defeated

SAM LUNGED AT GAIA'S LEGS, hoping to tackle her, to cover her body with his own. He should have known better. She simply jumped headfirst in the opposite direction, somersaulting gracefully over him. He threw his arms around empty space and struck the hard dirt.

"What are you *doing*?" she demanded.

"Quiet!" Sam whispered, ignoring the pain of hitting

the ground. His head spun in all directions as he surveyed the foliage for the gunman. *There!* Two men in camouflage jackets were kneeling in the bushes. One of them had a pistol. They were about twenty yards away. One of them lifted his head and—

"Will you get up?" Gaia demanded.

Two powerful hands clamped around Sam's biceps and yanked him to his feet. God, she was strong. He struggled to keep looking at the gunmen, but Gaia spun him around so that they were face-to-face.

"Why did you just try to tackle me?" she spat, breathing hard.

Sam could only shake his head. There was no way he could answer. Terror had rendered him mute. But he was finally beginning to understand. They'd wanted him to see them. Sam knew it. They wanted him to know—*two more minutes with her and you're both dead.* It was his final warning. It was a mandate, and Sam was too weak to fight it. He'd had enough chances to tell her the truth. And he'd screwed them up with indecision and jealousy and, most of all, cowardice. He was out of options.

"I don't know why," he forced himself to say, overcome with nausea. He glanced over his shoulder—and to his momentary relief, found that the gunmen had vanished. "I think it's because I'm so pissed at you. I mean, what are we really doing here, right? This will never work."

Gaia let him go. He nearly collapsed into the dirt.

"Excuse me?" she asked, her eyes narrowing.

But he could only scan her face for signs of that glowing red dot. It didn't seem to be there. Maybe the assassins had repositioned themselves. Maybe they were aiming from behind now. Or more than likely, there was more than one pair. He barely even noticed as Gaia shook her head and withdrew from him, her features contorting in anger.

"I think I better go," Sam said shakily. No doubt they were watching his every movement. They could probably hear his every word. He bit his tongue, dreaming of shoving their faces in the dirt for what they'd done to him. If only he knew what their faces looked like.

"Fine," Gaia said. There was no sigh, no hint of resignation. Just a single, cold word. "You know, you should have just done this weeks ago, Sam. It could have saved us both a long nightmare."

Her harsh monotone was like a quick swipe from a jagged knife, all the more painful because she was absolutely right. He *could* have saved them both a long nightmare. He didn't want to hear any more. He wanted the conversation to end. Before he lost it completely. Before he got them both shot.

"You're right," Sam said, falling into a defeated, bitter tone of his own. He started backing away from her, his eyes darting to the left and right. Paul and his friends were closing in.

"Who are you?" Gaia asked, her eyes brimming with tears. "I don't even know you. What do I really know about you, Sam? I don't even know where you are half the time. Because you won't tell me. And you know what? That proves that you don't know me very well. Because if you did know me at all, Sam, you'd know that whatever the hell is going on with you, I could handle it. If you really knew me, you'd know what I was. . ."

Sam forced himself to turn and run before she could finish, leaping through the rocks and the grass in the direction of downtown. He found that he didn't feel particularly sorrowful or even that angry. Instead he just felt. . . odd. It was a very disconcerting feeling to have nothing—not even to own your own life.

But it was liberating, too. Because now he was certain that he had nothing left to lose.

HEATHER STUMBLED ON HER WAY up the stairs, her legs wobbling with every step. Her shoulders had never felt so heavy. Maybe guilt could weigh a person down. If that was true, Heather wasn't sure she would make it out the door.

Fake a Seizure

Just a few more minutes, she thought, trying to soothe herself. *You'll get through this.*

Coming to this brunch had been a stupid, stupid mistake. But Heather had hoped to prove something to Ed. She'd hoped to show him that they could hang out with her friends from the Hamptons and still be a strong couple. Her alliance would remain with him. That was the difference between then and now.

She wasn't sure how she'd show it to him. All she knew was that she couldn't live with the shame anymore—the shame of those hours and minutes leading up to the accident. Because she knew now that she'd viewed him the way that they viewed him, as somebody who didn't quite measure up, for whatever reason. She'd bought into their foolish elitism so much that she'd ended up. . . doing what she did.

Don't think about that now. If you think about that now, you'll never get through the next five minutes.

Unfortunately, she nearly slammed headfirst into Chad when she reached the top of the stairwell.

"Are you all right?" he asked.

"I . . ." Heather swallowed. She could only nod. She was beginning to feel horribly dizzy. Brunch would have been so easy if Chad hadn't shown up. How could he even show his face, knowing Heather would be there? He was such an insensitive, arrogant son of a bitch. He was actually about to confess their secret to Ed just to get it off his chest. It was probably just some pointless little guilty tidbit to him—just some speck on his conscience that he felt compelled to floss. He probably had no idea what his confession would do to her. And to her relationship with Ed. And to her reputation in general.

"Well, I'm going to take a leak," he muttered, brushing past her.

Heather simply watched him go, her mouth hanging open. She wanted to scream at him to stop, but the words wouldn't come. He was going to run into Ed. And she couldn't let that happen. Not now, not ever. She'd cry if she had to—scream, fake stomach problems, fake a seizure, pull a fire alarm; she didn't care if she never saw these people again. But Chad was not going to have the chance to finish his confession—

The bathroom door closed behind him.

ED BALANCED HIS BODY AGAINST the rim of the sink and doused his face with cold water for the third time. Anything he could do to shake off the miserable tension Heather had created, to wash away the sight of Chad Carmel and this entire debacle that "normal" people called brunch. But when

Ping-Pong

he raised his head for a view of his dripping face in the fluorescent blue of the mirror, he felt like he was being stalked. Chad's reflected face was directly behind his shoulder, working his hair furiously to retrieve the perfect swoop and dangle.

"Hey," Chad mumbled. Somehow he was capable of making even one syllable offensive.

"Hey," Ed replied, opting for the simple response instead of the long version. *Hey, asshole. Thanks for turning my girlfriend into a raving lunatic. Now, get away from me before I ram this crutch so far down your throat, you'll have a permanent third leg.*

"Is Heather okay?" he asked.

What do you care, you just-in-from-the-Hamptons piece of shit? No, Heather's not okay. She's lost in your shallow materialistic world, and when she's around scum like you, she's ashamed to be seen with me. Plus she's on the verge of a total breakdown for no reason I can understand.

"Yeah, she's fine," Ed said.

"You sure? She doesn't look so hot."

"Yeah."

"Oh."

"I think I'm just going to take her home."

"Good idea."

The sound of their conversation reminded Ed of Ping-Pong. It had the same dull, repetitive tone. There was no real exchange. Words were just being swatted back and forth.

Chad leaned a half inch from the mirror and examined his pearly smile from all possible angles. Then he splashed his entire face and head with water and began a complete redesign of the hair.

"Have a nice day," Ed muttered. He tossed his towel into the trash and repositioned himself on his crutches. Then he reached for the door.

"Hold on," Chad commanded. "I just. . . wanted to say something to you."

Ed frowned at him. He couldn't imagine what kind of idiocy Chad would have to offer. He turned and faced the guy, expecting to see that painful hipster-wanna-be grin. But Chad looked unusually serious. Which was actually pretty comical, considering his head was dripping with water.

"I just—I just. . . ," Chad stammered, looking down at the floor. "I mean. . . now that you're going to be okay—you are going to be okay, right?"

"I hope so," Ed replied. "What are you talking about?"

Chad hesitated before speaking again. "Well, now that I've run into you again. . . and you're going to be okay. . . it just seemed like a chance to tell you. . . I'm sorry."

Oh, Jesus. Somehow this day had gotten even more surreal and agonizing. "Sorry for what?" Ed asked.

"For the whole master-bedroom thing," Chad said.

Ed stared at him with a slightly bemused smile. "I have no idea what you're talking about."

"The master-bedroom thing," Chad repeated. "The dare."

A strange sensation suddenly gripped Ed's stomach. He felt like his intestines were slowly being squeezed with a pair of tongs. And he wasn't even sure why. But his instincts were telling him that this was very, very bad. That it was going to hurt. And that it had something to do with Heather.

"You're going to have to be more specific," Ed stated. His voice quavered.

"Heather didn't tell you?"

Obviously not, you idiot. Ed shook his head.

Chad seemed confused. He scratched his chin. "Well, I didn't really know you, you know? When you came up to my house that weekend . . ."

"Uh-huh?" Ed prompted him.

"Yeah, so. . . I thought you were, you know. . . just kind of this skater dude or something. . . and I had to figure out which bedroom everyone was going to stay in, you know? So, since I really didn't know you, I was going to have you and Heather sleep in the tent."

Ed blinked. "The tent?" he repeated. He almost laughed. Each word out of Chad's mouth was more offensive than the next. He might as well have said "the servants' quarters" or "the doghouse" or "the dungeon." The guy never failed to outdo himself.

"Don't worry, it had a heater," Chad added.

"Thank you," Ed said dryly. "Okay, so a tent. I love camping out. You're forgiven. I'm glad we had this talk, Chad." He took another hobbling step toward the door.

"No, wait, but that's the thing," Chad insisted.

Ed paused and hung his head, dropping between his two crutches. "What's the thing?" he said with a groan.

"Heather didn't love camping out," Chad said. "She was all like, 'Heather Gannis does not sleep in a tent. Just for that. . . I want the master bedroom.' So I was like, there's no way you and the skater dude are getting the master bedroom. But she was like, what do I have to do to get the master bedroom? And I kept telling her to forget it, but I swear, man, she would not leave it alone. . . ."

The more Chad spoke, the more Ed felt like his brain had begun to swell. He couldn't stand it anymore; the pressure was too intense. But at the same time he didn't want Chad to stop, either. Ed's heart began to pound. His lungs heaved. He was curiously fascinated, though—much the way Chad and all the others must have been when they saw Ed's twisted body on the side of the road. Talk about sado-masochism at its finest. Why didn't he just open the door and get the hell out of here? They were in a goddamn *bathroom,* no less.

"She would not let it go," Chad continued, "no matter how many times I told her she couldn't have it. I swear, it was like she couldn't live unless she got that master bedroom. So finally I told her . . ." His voice trailed off.

Ed waited. "Told her *what?*" he pushed, turning to glare at Chad.

"I told her . . ." Chad looked stricken. "I told her if her skater dude could take Bannon's Hill, then she could have the master bedroom."

All at once the pressure vanished. Just like that. Ed blinked at Chad, but he didn't feel a thing. Nada. This wasn't the way it was supposed to be. He was supposed to fly off in a fit of rage. To bash Chad's head in. To find Heather and smack her in the face. Someone had to pay. Someone *should* pay. (Somebody besides the skateboard company, that was.) Right? But Ed only felt numb. Maybe there were too many emotions at the same time, and they'd all melded into the same dull feeling. It was like what happened when too many colors mixed together. They all became brown. Shit colored.

"But I was just kidding," Chad went on. "I didn't think she could possibly take me up on it. I mean, Bannon's Hill on a skateboard? Come on."

"Yeah," Ed said faintly. "You gotta be nuts."

Chad's face whitened. He threw his hand up on his

head. "Oh, God. I didn't mean it like that, dude. I'm sorry—"

"It's okay," Ed interrupted. He turned back toward the door and pushed it open with his crutch.

"I just didn't think you'd really do it," Chad insisted, pleading with him. "I mean. . . I didn't think she'd really ask you to do it. I mean, just so she could have the stupid bedroom—"

The door swung shut, cutting Chad off in mid-sentence. The silence was sweet, welcome relief. But the nightmare wasn't over. Far from it. Because once again Ed found himself face-to-face with Heather in the little foyer. Right back where he started. She looked at him with a desperate, almost crazed glint in her eye. And now, at last, he understood why.

"Hi," he said politely.

Heather smiled, but this time the veneer was just too thin. It couldn't mask the lies, the self-absorbed panic. "Hi. I just wanted to make sure everything was okay. What's going on?"

"We were just talking," Ed said. "It wasn't—"

The door crashed open behind him, slamming into his back and nearly sending him toppling to the floor. He fell against Heather, who somehow managed to support his weight. After a few grunts he regained his balance. She held on to his arm, but he shook free of her loose grip. Her hand fell away. Chad stood there, breathing heavily. He glanced at her.

"What were you talking about?" Heather mur-mured.

Ed just shook his head. He couldn't even bear to look at her anymore. It wasn't that he blamed her. He knew very well that she didn't deserve his blame. Not all of it, anyway. The bottom line remained the same: the accident was *his* fault. After all, he had agreed to go along with the stupid dare when he could have put his foot down. He could have said no. What was the worst that could have happened? He would look like a wimp to a bunch of stuck-up brats? They had already labeled him. No stunt, no matter how crazy or stupid, would have changed their opinion. It *didn't*. To them, he was still just a "skater dude."

But he couldn't forgive two years of deception. He couldn't forgive the fact that Heather had kept this terrible secret from him all this time, when he deserved her honesty. He deserved the raw, unadulter-ated truth. No matter how much it hurt. Because he couldn't love her if he didn't trust her. He couldn't even *like* her. Trust and love were inextricably bound together. One couldn't exist without the other. They were like water and oxygen. Without them, a relation-ship would die. Period.

"What were you talking about?" Heather repeated. The question was barely a whisper.

"About the fact that you had to have the master

bedroom," Ed said.

Heather swallowed. Her eyes began to well with tears. "You know, I figured Chad would say something to you. And I wanted to stop him. . . I wanted to stop him so badly." Her voice broke. "But I think, on some level, I also wanted you to hear the truth, so I let him go in there—"

"Shhh." Ed placed his finger over his lips. She didn't seem to be able to move. She blinked. Tears fell from her cheeks. There was no more to be said. Ed hobbled toward the stairs, then paused and glanced over his shoulder at the two of them. "Just so you know, for the record, I hate khakis," he announced. "No matter what may happen to me in this life, I will never again, for as long as I live, wear a pair of khakis. Thank you."

With that, Ed forced his way up the steps and walked out of Sarabeth's. He wondered what he'd do first in his life without Heather. It was very sunny out.

The mere sight
of the man
standing before
her had the
exact same

sanctuary

effect as being
thrown into the
middle of deadly
combat. Without
warning.

GAIA SAT ON THE DEEP WINDOWSILL, her arms wrapped tightly around her knees, staring from Mary's bedroom down at the Manhattan night. With the overload of thoughts in her head, she'd somehow missed the moment when it turned from day to night. In the daylight Central Park had looked like a vibrant green forest in the middle of the gray city. Now it looked more like a gaping black hole in the center of civilization. How appropriate.

Shut Up, Move On

"Do you want to talk about it?"

"Huh?" Gaia turned and saw Paul standing in the doorway. She hadn't even noticed he was there. For all she knew, he could have been standing there for hours, just looking at her. "I . . ," she began, but then she bowed her head. A deep sigh flowed from her lungs.

Did she want to talk about it?

Actually, no. She didn't. Not now, not ever. Her honest hope was never to talk about Sam Moon again. In fact, she was aiming for something deeper and more profound than that. Her ultimate goal was never to *think* about Sam Moon again. Wouldn't that just be a dream come true? *Sam who? Sam Moon? Oh, yeah, you mean that beautiful guy I went out with for about a day? Man, didn't he turn out to be a complete asshole? I can barely remember him!*

That was the plan. To forget him altogether.

Unfortunately, however, Gaia had a photographic memory. She could remember what she had for breakfast on October 10, 1992—the last of the strawberry Pop-Tarts in the box. Her father had eaten one and put the open pouch back in. She hated that. So, okay, forgetting Sam (or her father, too, for that matter) was pretty much out of the question.

But she could control her thoughts. She certainly wouldn't think about him. Because if she did, she might start to consider what they had gone through to be together—only to end up with this. Meaning nothing. She might start to think about the first day they met at the chess tables. Or that love letter, that stupid love letter. She'd do anything in the world to destroy that right now. What was worse than leaving all that naive vulnerability in his hands for eternity?

There was no point in asking that question, though. Because she wasn't thinking about him.

"No," she said suddenly, surprising herself. "I don't want to talk about it."

Paul walked into the room and sat at the foot of the bed. "Come on. Let me do something to help." He offered a tentative smile—that crooked grin that reminded Gaia so much of Mary. "Aren't we supposed to do something completely spontaneous and random now?"

Gaia laughed miserably. She turned again toward the dark window, looking past her ghostly reflection. "I think that plan has backfired," she mumbled.

"I'm sorry," Paul breathed.

"For what?" Gaia asked.

"For pissing Sam off," he said.

Gaia shook her head and glanced at him. "It has nothing to do with you. That's what I can't figure out. Something happened to him. I can't explain it. It was like. . . he lost something. Like his spirit or his soul or whatever got sucked out of him—not that I believe in any of that bullshit, but. . . you know, why am I talking about him? Shut up, Gaia. Move on, Gaia." She smiled grimly. "That's my new motto, Paul: Shut up, Gaia. Move on, Gaia. What do you think?"

Paul stared down at his shoes. "I think it's depressing," he whispered.

"Now you're catching on," Gaia said. She meant the comment to be wry, but it came out as nothing more than bitterly sarcastic. She bit her lip. She didn't want to torture Paul with her problems. But somehow she didn't think she'd be able to help herself. Not tonight.

"Maybe a good family dinner will help," Paul said.

Gaia nodded. "Dinner would be great," she said in a faraway voice. She knew she didn't sound sincere, but she was. At least she had a safe place to lick her wounds. The thought of having to go back to that empty apartment on Mercer Street or to George Niven's house on Perry Street. . . that was far too dark. Blacker than Central Park at night. Too dark even for Gaia Moore. No, she was not going to take this place for granted. This was her sanctuary.

"I think Olga's making goulash tonight," Paul said. "It's really good—"

The doorbell rang.

Paul frowned. "I wonder who that is."

"Is Brendan coming home tonight?" Gaia asked.

He shook his head, then stood up from the bed and headed out to the hall. "I don't think so. . . ."

Gaia bowed her head again. Maybe controlling her thoughts was easier said than done. Because she found herself wishing that the person ringing that doorbell was Sam. She slipped off the windowsill and stepped into the bathroom, where she splashed some cool water on her face. *"This will never work,"* he'd said, with barely a hint of emotion on his face. Screw him. Gaia pounded her fists down on the sink. Shut up, Gaia. Move on, Gaia. She flipped off the faucet and dried her face, trying to make herself presentable for dinner. The better she looked, the fewer questions they'd ask. One nice family dinner. At least an hour of peace—

"Gaia?" Mrs. Moss called from the front hall. "You have a guest."

Her heart plummeted.

Sam. She stared back at her own shocked face. Her wish had come true. Her awful, twisted wish. . . she hated him with all her heart. She never wanted to see him again. But she knew that if he said something true this time, if he managed to remind them both of who they were when all this started. . . she would forgive him. It was that simple. She wasn't that strong.

Squelching her strong impulse to run, she forced herself to walk—very slowly and deliberately. Her footsteps were soft on the hall carpet. She kept her head down, her face expressionless. She didn't even look up until she reached the living room.

And then she froze.

At that moment she felt like her bloodstream had been connected to an electric generator. Every part of her body tensed with its current. The mere sight of the man standing before her had the exact same effect as being thrown into the middle of deadly combat. Without warning. There was no fear as she took in his dark eyes, his slightly graying hair, his impeccably tailored and pressed suit. Of course not. There was no fear. . . only readiness. And wonder. And rage.

"You never told us you had an uncle," Mrs. Moss said, smiling at her.

THE MESSENGER WAS ALMOST TOO LATE.

Tom had already cleared customs at Frankfurt International Airport; his bags were checked through to New York.

Failed Operation

The flight was due to board at any minute. He was sitting at the bar near the gate, trying to relax with a glass of red wine, when the woman appeared at his side.

"I think you dropped your cell phone, sir," she murmured.

Tom didn't make eye contact with her. He didn't want to see her face. He simply nodded as she placed the slender black phone on the bar next to his glass, dread consuming him.

"Thank you," he said.

And then she was gone.

He was certain he wouldn't make it on that plane. Of course not. He clenched his teeth as he paid for his drink and hurried toward the rest room. It wasn't a secure location, but it would have to do. The phone rang even before he managed to push open the door.

"Yes?" he answered, scanning the stalls for any potential eavesdroppers. The room was empty. He was alone.

"Three, zulu, alpha, four, seven," an unrecognizable voice replied. It was the code for a failed operation.

Tom's pulse quickened. "Advise," he breathed.

"The toy store was a decoy. Loki has slipped his tail. Flight is canceled. Come to the restaurant."

For a moment Tom couldn't speak. The impact of the news was almost too overwhelming. The "toy store" was an illegal weapons factory deep in the Sudanese desert—specifically, one that manufactured anthrax. All intelligence seemed to indicate that Loki's latest venture involved the selling of biological weapons, particularly when the informant had mentioned DNA. But if Loki had led the agency on a wild-goose chase, if the anthrax was a decoy. . . then Tom and everybody else was completely in the dark about Loki's true intentions. He'd pulled the hardest trick possible in their deadly business. He'd managed a surprise.

"Come to the restaurant," the voice repeated.

"Understood," Tom forced himself to respond. His voice trembled. He clicked off the phone and dropped it into the garbage, then hurried from the rest room.

Until this very moment, Tom had never considered that Gaia might actually play a role in whatever Loki had planned. He'd simply assumed that Loki wanted Gaia for himself—to serve him for whatever vile purposes, to exploit her many talents. But now he wasn't so sure. He wasn't so sure at all. The informant had said something about her, right before he mentioned the DNA. . . .

That wasn't what terrified him the most, though. What terrified him the most was that Loki had managed to shake his surveillance.

He could be anywhere at this moment. Anywhere.

"HELLO, GAIA," OLIVER SAID.

Victim

He was standing between Mr. and Mrs. Moss and Paul. Near enough to touch them. Gaia clenched her fists at her sides. Here she was, face-to-face with the man who'd killed her mother. But she knew he wouldn't try to harm her. Or them. If he had wanted the Mosses out of the picture, they'd already be dead. Of that she was certain.

"What do you want?" Gaia whispered, fighting to control her voice.

Oliver laughed. The Mosses exchanged uncomfortable smiles. "I'm sorry to barge in on you like this, without calling first," he apologized. "But I'm just about to leave the country, and I just wanted to say good-bye."

Gaia nodded. "Fine. Good-bye."

The smiles on the faces of Paul and his mother began to fade.

But Oliver simply laughed again. "I was hoping we could talk somewhere privately for a moment." He glanced at the Mosses. "Again, I'm sorry. I won't be long. I promise."

Both Paul and Mrs. Moss looked expectantly at Gaia.

"Okay," Gaia murmured. She had to hand it to him: coming here was a brilliant move on his part—to trap her someplace where she'd feel safe. Where she wouldn't try to run and where she couldn't kill him. Without another word, Gaia turned and marched back to Mary's bedroom. Oliver followed a few paces behind her. Only in a cold and sweaty nightmare could Gaia have imagined being in this house with. . . *him*. With Loki. Yes, she could no longer think of him as her uncle Oliver. The notion of being related to him was too sickening.

She threw open the door and marched to the window.

For several long seconds neither of them spoke. Loki closed the door behind him. "You look stunning," he said, standing by the foot of the bed.

Gaia kept her gaze fixed to the glass, to the winking lights of the East Side, across the park. Somehow it made such perfect sense that he was there—like a vulture that had just been waiting to swoop in once the carnage of her life was complete. How had he timed his entrance so perfectly?

"Say what you have to say and leave," she hissed.

Loki breathed out a small sigh. "My God, he really has totally brainwashed you. I want you to know I have people looking for him right now, Gaia. He's going to pay for what he's done, I promise you."

Gaia rolled her eyes. "What are you talking about?"

"Gaia, look at me, please," he begged. "I can't talk to you like this. I can't stand what he's done to you. Please, look at me."

She shook her head but turned to him—if for no other reason than just to shut him up and get on with this. But when she met his gaze, she realized that she wasn't in danger of losing her temper. She was far more in danger of succumbing to the sadness she'd been desperately trying to keep at bay for the last forty-eight hours. Because as repellent as Loki was to her, he had the same eyes as her father. Only the love there was false. Just as her father's had been.

"Just tell me why you're here," she said deliberately, "and leave."

"I'm here because I love you, Gaia," he said. "I'm here because my brother has told you some horrible lies. I have to set the record straight, if only for myself. To be honest, I don't know if you're capable of believing the truth at this point or not."

Believe. Truth. Honest. These were not words that Gaia had any desire to hear again today. She was so tired of trying to discern the truth. Too tired.

"I don't want to do this," she murmured.

"Gaia, just hear me out, please. Don't you see what Tom's doing? Do you even know where he is right now? Did he even tell you where—"

"I don't want to talk about him," Gaia interrupted, straining every muscle in her body to maintain her composure.

"He's in Germany. I had him followed. He's not who he claims to be, Gaia. He's meeting with some very frightening people. Why wouldn't he tell you where he was going? Why wouldn't he have contacted you once? Because he doesn't want you to know. You can see the logic."

"Doesn't want me to know what?" Gaia snapped.

"He doesn't want you to know that he is Loki."

Gaia's eyes narrowed. She didn't know whether to laugh or to scream—or to rip that phony, pleading look from his face with her bare hands and leave him in a bloody heap on the floor.

"Excuse me?" she asked.

He nodded. "You have to let me protect you."

"I can protect myself," she shot back.

"Not from Loki, you can't."

"I'm doing a pretty good job right now, aren't I?" she asked, folding her arms in front of her. "Try something. Go ahead. Just try something. You'll be very sorry. . . *Loki*."

"I'm not—"

"Shut up!" she shouted, her eyes blazing. "You're Loki. I know you are!"

But her uncle just shook his head, very sadly. "That's what my brother wants you to believe. He's been passing himself off as the 'good' brother. He's been playing the part of me to throw people off his trail—to throw you off his trail. He's tried to convince you that I'm him—that I'm Loki so that you won't trust me, so that I can't protect you. Don't you understand?"

Gaia fell silent. The truth of the matter was that she didn't understand and that she was no longer interested in *trying* to understand. Her mind could no longer process what she was hearing. She was simply an empty vessel through which words passed.

Her uncle moved a step closer. "Gaia, think back now," he pleaded quietly. "Please. Think back through everything that's happened. I tried to take you away with me to Europe—to save you from all this, to save you from him, and what did he do? He tricked you into getting on a plane with him. And he had me put in jail just to be sure I couldn't get to you. He probably tried to convince you that I killed Katia, but if you only knew . . ." His voice quavered. He reached for the handkerchief tucked in his jacket and dabbed his eyes with it.

Gaia stared at him. She felt nauseated. This display of emotion was extremely disturbing, to say the least. If he was faking this, he was an extremely gifted actor. Not that she should be surprised. If there was one thing she was truly certain of, it was that people had a tremendous capacity for lying.

"I loved your mother so dearly," he went on. He sniffed and folded the handkerchief. "I did everything in my power to protect her from your father. I tried so many times to warn her. But I failed. He took her from us both, Gaia. . . . And then he fled, that coward. Don't you see? You've got to put the pieces together yourself. Don't waste your time trying to figure out which one of us is more credible. That's impossible. Given all the emotional complications, you'd drive yourself insane trying to determine the truth that way."

In spite of the venom coursing through Gaia's veins, she found she couldn't argue with him. It was the truest thing she had heard anyone say in days. She yearned to be coldhearted again. To feel nothing again. To make her decisions based entirely on facts and reason and give her heart a long and much needed rest. Maybe even a permanent rest. But right now her heart was still in overdrive, beating too much and then too little, and then not at all, and then too much again. And Oliver was only feeding the flame. Gaia had not a clue where her alliances were anymore. Not a clue.

"Please just consider this," he said softly. "If our track records can count for anything, consider the facts. Tom has abandoned you twice. Disappeared into thin air with no warning, no concern whatsoever for your welfare. I have now come back for you twice—to rescue you. And I'm asking you once more. Let me protect you. Let me take you to Europe, as we'd planned before. Let me take you away from Loki. I've seen what he could do to his wife. I can't sit back and watch him do it to his daughter as well." His voice hardened, and he stuffed his handkerchief back into his breast pocket. "I will not allow that to happen."

Gaia hung her head. She was too weak to respond. Every sentence was another debilitating blow. He was a skilled martial artist—so skilled, he only needed to use words to render her useless. The fight had gone out of her.

"I can see that your surrogate family here is wonderful," he said, with a warm smile. "You don't know how grateful I am to them for taking care of you. But you deserve a real family. A family that wants you. That is the most precious gift in the world. There's no substitute for that. Because you and I are the same, Gaia. You and me and your mother. We've all been victims of Tom. But if we leave here together, we won't have to be victims anymore. I know you want that as badly as I do—to stop being a victim."

"Yes." Gaia was hardly aware that she had spoken. The word seemed to appear magically before her, hovering there between them like a miniature star. She *did* want to stop being a victim. The problem was, she had no idea who was doing the victimizing anymore. Loki or Tom or Oliver. . . they were all the same. They all abused her, in one form or another—whether they had intended to or not.

"I've said too much," he offered gently. "I'm sorry. I'll leave you alone now." He walked toward the door but stopped himself and looked calmly at her, his eyes still reddish. "I'd never try to decide anything for you.

Only you know what you truly believe. But know this. Know that you have a real family. One that would never abandon you. One that would always try to protect you."

He reached into his front coat pocket and pulled out a card, which he placed on the bureau beside the mirror. "You can reach me at that number anytime."

Gaia stared at the floor. *Just go now,* she pleaded silently. *Now, before I make an ass of myself and start crying. Please.*

"Thank you for hearing me out," he said. "Whether you believe me or not. . . I love you, Gaia. I know it's true even if you don't. Good night."

He closed the door behind him. Gaia listened as he said good-bye to the Mosses and left the apartment. She didn't move—not for a very, very long time. She stood perfectly still. Because she was pretty sure that whichever foot she used to take the first step would be the wrong one.

I can hardly comprehend the extent to which my life has come full circle. I mean, I'm literally right back where I started. It's like my entire relationship with Sam and the entire reunion with my father were just little shadow plays to amuse me while I continued my descent into the underworld. That's where I reside now. That's where my proverbial ship has landed.

You know what it's like? It's like Sam and my father turned to stone. Like the Greek myth of Medusa. I always thought Medusa was so cool, what with snakes for hair, but apparently she was just so ugly that she turned people to stone. And that's what it feels like with Sam and my father. First, of course, I turned them into my heroes. They became the two biggest figures in my life, golden gods, models of true love and true family and perfection.

And then something went terribly

wrong. I don't really understand
where or how it happened—or what
even caused the trouble. But the
next thing I knew. . . my heroes
had turned to stone. That's all
they are to me now. Just these
oversized lifeless white statues.
Reminders of heroes past. Hollow,
brittle tributes to what I thought
they were. What they were supposed
to be.

And that's not the worst of
it. Because they didn't just
turn to stone. . . they crum-
bled, falling down all over me
in an avalanche of arms and
noses and legs. Now I'm sub-
merged in the rubble. Buried
under all their bullshit. Trying
to pry my way out.

I miss Ed. I wish I could talk
to Ed. But maybe Ed isn't real,
either. Maybe he's just a shell,
too. Or an actor who was just
pretending to be in a wheelchair.
That's how it felt. It felt like
he had been my favorite character
in my favorite movie—and then

the actor who played him walked
into school, and I knew it was
the same guy, but it just wasn't
the same guy.

I'm starting to sound like a
bona fide lunatic. I know that.
I've been watching it get worse
and worse. But I swear to God,
I'm sane. It's my life that's
insane: a surreal tapestry made
up of lies and phantoms and shadows and hollow statues.

And looking out from under all
the rubble, I can't help thinking. . .

Maybe my uncle Oliver is the
only thing that's real.

It's a strange thing about choices. People always like to think they're making them, when in fact they are not. They like to think they're deciding which movie to see, or which orange juice to buy, or where they'll be taking their next vacation. And they are truly unaware that pages and pages of demographic studies, and tests, and focus groups have predetermined their "choices" long before they even get to the stage where they can decide. They are blissfully ignorant of being manipulated by a machine much, much larger than they.

Of course, I think that in some part of their subconscious mind, they have an awareness of the fact that they're being "helpfully guided" through life by powers far superior to them. I think they need that guidance. I think they'd feel completely lost at sea without it.

Gaia needs my guidance right now. Just as she needs to feel

that she has chosen to seek it out. She'll make her choice as to whether or not she's going to join me abroad, not understanding that the choice has already been made. All according to a plan.

Control. There are so many misconceptions about it. All this foolishness about how there's no such thing. People love to convince themselves that they have some kind of free will and that this free will plays any roll in their choices. It's really quite ridiculous. But I am eternally grateful for the illusion.

Because the illusion of free will is the one essential element in maintaining complete control.

F E A R L E S S

They say that old habits die hard.

  I have to agree.

    Just look at my father.

He still hasn't kicked the habit of
abandoning me.

But that's alright.

Because if he can run . . . so can I.